What Happened to Liz

Crysta Duryea

Copyright © 2026 by Crysta Duryea
All rights reserved.

ISBN: 979-8-9945379-0-9
Published by Deacon Rose Publishing

No part of this book may be reproduced, stored in a retrieval system, or transmitted in any form or by any means—electronic, mechanical, photocopying, recording, or otherwise—without prior written permission of the author, except for brief quotations used in reviews.

This is a work of fiction. Names, characters, places, and events are either the product of the author's imagination or are used fictitiously. Any resemblance to actual persons, living or dead, or actual events is purely coincidental.

First edition.

For my little family.
Your love carried me here.
Davey, I love you forever.

Crysta Duryea

Author's Note:
Just a quick note for friends and family: this book is completely fictional. The characters are not based on real people, and any similarities are coincidental. Please enjoy the story as imagination and storytelling—nothing personal, nothing intentional. Thank you so much for reading.

Author's Note 2:
Repeatedly asking the author "what happened to Liz" will not speed up the answer. Only reading to the end will. "Coral Haven" appears 95 times in this book. Yes, I looked it up. Yes, it's a lot. Sorry not sorry. Welcome to town.

People keep asking, *"What happened to Liz?"*

And honestly?
I could tell you…

But where's the fun in that?

You'll have to turn the pages like everyone else.
Mwahaha.

Prologue

I coasted down Beach Street on my black-and-brown beach cruiser barefoot, the same one I'd rescued from the town thrift shop last spring. The wicker basket rattled with my recycled canvas tote and an iced coffee I should've finished before leaving, but I didn't mind. The chain squeaked, the sea breeze tugged at my messy bun, and the whole town was already stretching awake.

Families were unloading their cars in front of the pastel rental cottages that lined the road. Luggage thudding onto sidewalks, beach chairs clattering, boogie boards stacked like bright plastic shields. Someone's shih tzu barked furiously at a passing golf cart. A kid trailed behind his parents, clutching a half-inflated flamingo float, already crying before ten a.m.

Summer had officially started moving in.

I pedaled toward the Jackson Street beach entrance, where the first round of beach tags were being sold from a small wooden kiosk. The teenage tagger running the stand couldn't have been older than fifteen. His Coral Haven Beach Patrol T-shirt was two sizes too big, and the brim of his cap was ratty and bleached pale by the sun.

"Morning," I said. "How's it going? Big crowd already?"

He squinted at me through the glare. "Not bad for a weekday. It's the tourists that keep me having fun; they move in like they're here forever. Three coolers, a bajillion beach towels, and an entire pantry in their trunks." He grinned and chuckled to himself. "You missed the big thing earlier, though."

"Oh yeah?" I balanced one foot on the sand, letting my other cool off from the heat. "What'd I miss?"

He leaned an elbow on the counter, lowering his voice like he was about to share classified information. "The fudgie wudgie guys went at it again. Right on the beach path. Full shouting match, ice cream flying, sprinkles everywhere. One of 'em even threw a cone. It was so close from hitting this chubby kid."

I blinked and smirked. "No way. A cone?"

"Chocolate," he said gravely. "Waste of a good scoop and good money."

I laughed, shaking my head. "You sure you're not totally making this up?"

"Swear on my beach badge," he said, holding it up proudly. "You can probably still see the melted ice cream near the lifeguard stand."

"Good to know," I said, pushing off again. "I'll keep an eye out for evidence."

As I pedaled away, the laughter faded behind me. An ice cream war between two old men was hilarious news. The sun caught the ocean's tide and sparkled just beyond the dunes.

How quickly things can change and how quickly I came to realize that even the prettiest towns can hide something rotten just beneath the sand.

In just a few short weeks, an innocent woman would be dead, and the town would buzz with rumors, accusations, and half-truths, each one uglier than the last.

*

This Week on the Dunes: Get Ready, People!

The Calm Before the Buzz

You can always tell when Coral Haven starts waking up again. The mornings feel brighter, the air smells like excitement and paint thinner, and suddenly the parking lot outside Java Wave is full of shop owners with to-go lattes and anxiety.

Shops Dusting Off

Beach Street is officially shaking off the cobwebs for the 2007 summer season. Doors are open, windows propped, and someone somewhere is always dragging a broom across a wood floor. UPS and FedEx trucks are practically part of the scenery now, hauling boxes of candles, swimsuits, woven bags, cocktail syrups, and about a thousand "Now Open!" signs. If you see a driver, maybe give them a cold drink and a thank-you. They've earned it.

Locals to Know

If you need a hand getting your space ready, May Genuine is back and already booking out her commercial cleanings. Message me if you need her number—she's quick, discreet, and somehow makes even the worst winter grime disappear.

Around Town

The roads have been conveniently repaved just in time for bike season. Pedal Pelican has helmets on sale this week, so if your cruiser's been rusting in the shed since last Labor Day, now's your chance to look responsible while you ride.

Final Sip

The town's humming again, full of paint fumes and possibility. We're ready for the sunburns, the chaos, the small-town drama that'll unfold between Memorial Day and Labor Day. Same ocean, new stories.

Until next week,
—Claire Bear

ONE

My heart raced, my hands shook.

A low, restless dread settled into my chest.

The night before I left the city in 2005, a wave of uncontrollable nerves rushed through my body. My suitcase sat open on the floor, stuffed with sundresses that looked wildly out of place against my pressed blazers and trousers, with the city skyline glowing through the window.

Our 1,200-square-foot apartment was mostly empty. My things were in boxes stacked by the door, taped shut but still somehow leaking memories. The faint smell of takeout lingered: soy sauce, wasabi and ginger, and something that once was home.

I told myself this was what I wanted. A clean break with Deacon, a chance to breathe again. But standing there, staring out at the twinkle of traffic below, it didn't feel like freedom. It felt like failure.

Deacon's voice still echoed in my head from that last argument. *You're running away, Claire. You think the ocean's going to fix you?*

Maybe I was. Maybe it would. I didn't know anymore. All I knew was that every corner of this city reminded me of him, of us, of the version of me that waited for late-night texts, that marketed other people's stories instead of writing her own.

So I packed what I could fit in the back of my car: my laptop, my journals, two plants that probably wouldn't survive with me, and a box of half-finished drafts. Everything else, I left behind.

By sunrise, I was on the highway, the city shrinking in my rearview mirror until it was just a smudge of gray against the pink morning sky. The radio bustled with static between stations, and for a moment I almost turned back. But then I saw the first glint of water on the horizon, and something in my chest loosened.

I didn't know if I was chasing peace or just running from heartbreak, but either way, I kept driving.

The town was a dot on the map. A place I'd once written about in a freelance travel piece and promised myself I'd visit someday. I guess *someday* had finally arrived.

By the time I crossed the bridge into Coral Haven, the wind tangled through my hair like it already knew me. The ocean stretched out endlessly beside the road, shimmering like something alive.

I rolled down the window, took a deep breath, and whispered it aloud—

"New story."

Two Years Later

Two years can change everything—or at least convince you that starting over will.

If you drive about three hours south of the city, past the clogged highways and the suburbs that all look the same, you'll find Coral Haven, a picture-perfect beach town wrapped in salty air and secrets. Population 4,208. A place that smells like wildflowers and french fries, where every house has a name instead of a number and you're never more than a few blocks from the ocean or bay.

Moving here hadn't been part of my carefully laid life plan. But after the breakup and losing my marketing job in one of those sweeping "corporate restructurings," I needed a reset. The kind where you dramatically trade office noise for ocean waves.

I'd been good at my job. A senior marketing specialist before twenty-eight. A title that made your parents proud. But when the layoffs hit, the life I'd built around deadlines and promotions vanished overnight. I fell into a fog of self-doubt until I remembered the only part of that job that had ever made me feel alive. Storytelling.

Back in the city, I'd moonlighted as a blogger for a neighborhood newsletter, writing cheeky little blurbs about restaurant openings and community fundraisers. It wasn't glamorous, but I loved it. The sense of connection, the rhythm of a town talking to itself. When I moved to Coral Haven, I realized how much I missed that pulse.

Now, I rent a tiny purple bungalow with a crooked porch and a lemon tree that produces exactly two lemons a year. I waitress at The Driftwood on the north end of Beach Street and babysit for summer families. It's not glamorous, but it's perfect. I know the regulars, the shop owners, and the tourists who think the town belongs to them for a few months. I smile, I serve drinks, I listen.

And I write. Every night, under the dim light of my desk lamp, I slip into a world of storyboards, colorful characters, and children's book ideas I still promise myself I'll finish soon.

To fill the rest of my creative itch, I revived my old blogging habit. This time on Myspace, of all places. *This Week on the Dunes* became my friendly letter to Coral Haven: part gossip column, part community update section, part rumor blurb. Locals read it for the whispers, tourists for the charm. I write it because it keeps me sane.

My parents had been proud when I moved here. "It's about time you did something for yourself," Mom said. They worried I'd be lonely, but Coral Haven never let me be. Between café shifts and babysitting, my days were full. And my nights, somehow, fuller.

TWO

Everyone was talking, and not just about weather or parking tickets or who got a nose job over winter. No, today it was about local resident Bauer Clips and the grand opening of his new beach shop.

And his new out-of-towner girlfriend, Ava Delaney.

And the fact that their new shop is located just steps from the store Bauer and his ex-fiancée, Liz Carper, had run together for six years.

If you don't know Beach Street, picture a sun-drenched strip lined with more than forty beach shops and restaurants. Dilapidated signs, shell jewelry, overpriced shirts, and enough sage bundles to fumigate the Eastern Seaboard. Some stores are barely wider than a closet, but they do big business in the summer.

Liz's place, The Sand Dollar, has always been one of the best. Organized, maybe a little snobby. She sold handmade candles and dresses in soft sea-glass colors, each display immaculate. Locals liked her. Tourists loved her.

Bauer's new shop? No one even knows the name yet. Rumors say, "The Shore Thing." But it's opening. And it sells *very similar custom designs.* And Ava's been spotted arranging "coincidentally familiar" merchandise through the windows, swinging ponytail and all.

And that Liz is furious.

I strolled by the upcoming shop. The plywood boards were gone from the windows, replaced by a bright coat of white paint that still smelled like money and ambition. A "Grand Opening" banner flapped across the porch like a challenge.

Liz's store was open too, earlier than usual. Lights on, windows pristine, a new table display front and center. Ocean-scented candles, freshly ironed Coral Haven tees, and a framed sign that read:

Quality is silent. Loud is insecure.
I smirked. *Well played, Liz.*

*

This Week on the Dunes: Fresh Pies, Shark Surprises & Ice Cream Drama

Summer's officially stretching its toes in the sand—and so is our little town. Here's what's been stirring along the shoreline this week.

Beach Lady Farm Is Back in Bloom
Great news for all you fresh-produce lovers: Beach Lady Farm has reopened for the season! Their stands are brimming with crisp greens, sun-kissed tomatoes, juicy peaches, and—perhaps the true star—those famous key lime pies that somehow taste like sunshine wrapped in love. Locals are already lining up early to snag their favorites before noon. Don't wait too long; the pies have a way of disappearing fast.

A Shark Tale on Bay Beach

If you noticed a crowd gathering down by the bay beach this week, here's why: A tiger shark—yes, a tiger shark—washed up along the shore. The poor creature didn't make it, but the real spectacle came when the wildlife department arrived to handle the removal. Kids, cameras—it was the talk of the bay beach for hours. Some say it was the biggest shark they've seen up close in years. Nature has its wild ways of reminding us who really owns the water.

Ice Cream Wars Heat Up

What's summer without a little drama served cold? Our two beloved beach ice cream fudgie wudgie men—who've always kept their rivalry at a quiet simmer—finally let the tension boil over. Eyewitnesses say the two got into a heated shouting match right on the boardwalk, arguing over where they're allowed to sell their frozen treats. No punches, but plenty of words tossed like sprinkles. It's anyone's guess how this chilly turf war will settle.

Stay salty, friends. More whispers, more waves, more wonder to come.

—Claire Bear

THREE

Coral Haven liked to sell itself as a little gem of paradise.

A town that felt caught between centuries. The main stretch, blocks full of charm and chatter, was lined with old Victorian homes turned into stores. Their gables leaned like they'd spent too many years braving weather and carrying on the salt wind. Each one had its own personality: faded shutters, chipped green paint, curling flower boxes spilling with petunias. A few still had brass doorbells that jingled when you walked in.

Town was over three hundred years old, and the local preservation board made sure you never forgot it. Every storefront had to stay "historically accurate," which meant even the new smoothie shop operated out of a century-old clapboard cottage with slanted floors and painted-shut windows. In Coral Haven, progress had to hide behind charm.

Only two bridges led to the island. They were both narrow, both temperamental when the tide was high. When storms rolled in, you could almost hear the whole town holding its breath, waiting for the world to dry out again. Maybe that's why people here were so protective of routine. The ferry schedule. The morning bell from the lighthouse. The weekend farmers' market on Beach Street that clogged traffic and kept the tourists happy.

Horse-drawn carriages clattered down the cobblestone side streets, giving guided tours that no one really needed but everyone secretly loved. Kids waved from the sidewalks, and the drivers called out facts about shipwrecks, old sea captains, and "the ghost who still haunts room six at the Seabreeze Inn."

Even the landscaping seemed to glow with tradition. Spring brought pastel tulips and hydrangeas, summer meant overflowing window boxes and seashell planters, autumn brought pumpkins and cornstalks zip-tied to lampposts.

By the time the first ferry horn sounded, the gulls were already on patrol, and the shopkeepers were unlocking doors in a slow, synchronized rhythm. Hinges creaked, music drifted, and the sound of grinding coffee underpinned everything.

*

If you stood on Beach Street long enough, you could watch the whole town wake: surfers with boards under their arms, retirees in swim trunks walking dogs that always stopped at the same mailbox, and parents applying copious amounts of suntan lotion onto their wiggling spawn. Everything was familiar and temporary at once, as if Coral Haven existed only between Memorial Day and Labor Day.

Our little island was where rich people came to pretend they were "down to earth." There's no public transportation onto the island, which feels less like a coincidence and more like a gatekeeping strategy. The ferries are full of Range Rovers and Jaguars. Most of the summer crowd is made up of trust fund babies, big-city finance guys who compulsively check email on their BlackBerry, even on the beach, and old money types who call their housekeepers "part of the family."

Even the families I babysit for are *rich-rich*. Like, fresh-renovation-fume-still-in-the-air, everything-matching-Pottery-Barn rich. Their homes have ocean views, imported rugs, and artwork that looks like it belongs in a gallery, probably because it *does*. They all say they're "simplifying" by escaping the city. But their simple version involves $20,000 patio furniture and custom golf carts for their kids.

*

Before leaving the house for work, I'd caught my reflection in the mirror. Not out of vanity, just habit. My green eyes looked brighter than usual against the bit of mascara I'd swiped on, the only makeup I ever really bothered with, besides blush to sharpen my cheekbones. My hair had dried in loose, beachy waves from my shower, brushing the tops of my shoulders. The waitress outfit clung in a way that reminded me of the work I'd been putting in: the early runs, the late-night workouts, the quiet discipline that made me feel like I still had control over something. I wasn't the fragile version of myself I'd been when I first moved here. I'd built myself back into someone sturdy.

I grabbed my tote and took the long way to The Driftwood. The breeze off the dunes lifted the hem of my shirt and carried snippets of conversation from the pier: someone arguing about fish prices, a couple deciding between ice cream flavors at nine in the morning.

Still, there were mornings like this with the sunlight soft, air lofty, when I'd catch a glimpse of myself and wonder if anyone could tell how much effort it took to look effortless.

I had a few minutes to kill before my shift at The Driftwood, so I veered right off Beach Street and ducked into The Sand Dollar. My usual go-to spot to window-shop and browse.

The second I stepped through the door, the smell hit me: coconut, leather, and something soft and herbal that I couldn't name but instantly wanted to bathe in. Liz always said scent was half the sale. She was probably right.

I'd always liked Liz. She wasn't flashy or gaudy like some of the other boutique owners, just quietly zoned in. A motivated person who built her world one to-do list at a time. Work came first for her, always. The Sand Dollar wasn't just a store. It was her life's rhythm.

Most nights, her lights stayed on long after everyone else had closed. You'd pass by and see her through the window, hair in a loose bun, unpacking new shipments or rearranging displays that already looked perfect, all while drinking a few glasses of wine. She cared about everything. The scents, the clothes racks, the textures, the way customers felt when they walked in.

She didn't go out much anymore this past winter and spring, not since she'd started running the place alone. Introverted, maybe, but always easy to talk to. Liz had a calm presence, the kind that made you feel seen even in passing. She wasn't one for gossip or drama, she just *worked really hard.*

It made sense that her shop was always immaculate. Liz lived her life the way she ran The Sand Dollar: tremendously type A and every detail in its place.

Her boutique was filled with woven baskets full of gaudy scarves, macramé wall hangings, and linen dresses that somehow made you feel like a richer person just for touching them. Everything was neutral-toned and twice as expensive as it should be, but somehow totally worth it.

"Hi, welcome in—oh, hey Claire," Liz said from behind the counter, not even looking up from her laptop. "You're up earlier than usual."

"I have a breakfast shift," I said, running my hand along a rack of white and peachy-beige tops. "Figured I'd treat myself to something cute before I spend the morning covered in pancake syrup."

She smirked. "I'm not mad about it. Tell the other girls to stop by soon."

I pulled out a flowy cream-colored blouse with tiny embroidered sunflowers on the sleeves. "Of course. I know Carly will love this," I said. "Olivia is going to adore the tank tops with baby cats on them. And this is gorgeous," I said, as I pointed to another item.

"It's new," she said, finally looking up. She wore a sage-green wrap dress and her usual stacked gold rings. Her long brown hair was up in a low bun, but a few wispy pieces had slipped out, softening her pointed cheekbones. She obviously didn't realize how attractive she was. Liz's freckled face scrunched up as she checked her inventory, counting the sizes displayed on the racks. "Hand-dyed. Local artist. Only three in stock."

Sold.

"I'll take it. I just got paid. I'm trying to save my summer paychecks for winter vacations, but . . ." I said, draping it over my arm. "Consider it a really early birthday present to myself."

"Happy way early upcoming birthday. Isn't it at the end of the season?" she said, gleeful but confused, as she rang me up. "How old? Any ideas of what your birthday plans could be?"

"Thirty, ew. Kill me. Oh God, I have no idea. It is a few months out. Probably something big though, to celebrate the end of summer too. I think we might plan a casual backyard bash. You are more than welcome to come, Liz!" I said emphatically. Liz smiled and nodded in response.

As the card machine beeped, she glanced toward the front window and her entire expression changed. Just slightly. Her mouth puckered. Her eyes narrowed.

I turned to follow her gaze and saw Bauer's new shop across the street. The front door was propped open now, and Ava—blond, tan, and perfect—was positioning a stand of beach bags just outside. Music was already playing from a portable speaker, something upbeat and alternative, almost Hollister-esque.

The building sat low, its brick siding washed nearly white from years of salty air and relentless sun. A black door anchored the façade, its storm door cracked and hanging slightly crooked, like it had given up fighting the wind long ago. To the left, a three-panel window display faced the street.

"Oh," I said carefully. "So. That's actually happening."

Liz gave a dry little laugh and handed me my receipt. "Yep. That's the new version of me and my store, ha ha," she said, mockingly.

I raised an eyebrow without speaking, hoping she would dish more juicy information in my silence.

"My ex-fiancé," she clarified. "Bauer, you know. And the human Barbie over there is Ava Delaney. His new . . . slut piece, or whatever."

"I didn't realize—"

"No one did," she cut in, brisk but not bitter, and innocently shrugged. "We were engaged until December. He moved out right after New Year's. I heard he spent some time in LA, came back, and now he's opening that place with her less than six months later."

I didn't know what to say, so I didn't say anything. I just gave a sympathetic glance.

She tried to look carefree and unbothered, but her jawline was prominent. "It's fine. People can do whatever they want. It's a free country—and a free street, apparently."

I glanced back at Ava, who was now arranging locally designed pastel hats on a hook. To be fair, the display looked inviting; every product was placed deliberately. It was hard not to notice that they looked suspiciously similar to the ones Liz had started stocking last summer.

"Did he know you carried these kinds of pieces?" I asked gently.

"Oh, of course! The dick knew everything. We ran the store in tandem." She smiled without humor. "I guess he liked them enough to steal the whole idea."

She picked up a ceramic mug and began rearranging a shelf, suddenly busy. "Anyway. I'm not worried. People know quality. They know authenticity. I'm not going to let him just . . . copy and paste it."

I nodded, unsure if she was convincing me or herself.

"Enjoy the top," she added, forcing a smile. "You always pick good ones."

"Thanks," I said, and meant it. I turned on my heel and walked out the door.

Outside, the breeze lifted, warm and bright, carrying the sound of Ava's laugh and Bauer's voice as they greeted customers trickling in.

I could overhear some of the banter: "It's so good to see you again, Ryan!" Bauer said. "Yes, we are super stoked the store opened right on time for the season to begin! Thanks for checking us out. Come back ASAP, we'll have new brands soon."

FOUR

Coral Haven has its own way of telling stories.

No shocking exposés. Just quiet murmurs shared over iced lattes, knowing glances exchanged at crosswalks, and facts traded as casually as weather updates: low tide at noon, and a seventy percent chance of betrayal.

Merely half a year ago, Bauer Clips and Liz Carper were the town's golden couple. They grew up here—high school sweethearts with a first kiss on the boardwalk, prom photos in front of the lighthouse, the whole corny script. After graduation, they left Coral Haven together, finished college, and quickly found their way back home.

They opened The Sand Dollar in their twenties and ran it side by side for nearly six years, building something that felt as permanent as the tide. So when they got engaged, nobody was surprised. And when things finally started to go south, most of us never saw it coming.

She was the style. He was the strategy. She picked out the merchandise, made it beautiful and unique. He handled invoices and margins, knew how to talk to suppliers and set up the shipping accounts. He organized the bills, online orders, and tax documents. They were the couple people pointed at and said, "That's how you do it."

And then, something drastically changed.

Depending on who you asked, it was Liz who pulled away first. Or maybe it was Bauer who drifted. Rumor had it they'd been quietly unraveling for eight, maybe ten months. Long before anyone was willing to admit the engagement was off.

Some swore Bauer cheated. Others said Liz grew to hate him. A few blamed this new out-of-town girlfriend, insisting there had been an overlap, though no one ever saw anything concrete—just a look, maybe, or a conversation that lasted a little too long.

And then there were the people who said it was the store itself. Too many hours, too much stress, too much pride poured into something that stopped being *theirs* and started being *hers*. Liz kept The Sand Dollar. Bauer didn't.

What everyone agreed on was this: When they finally split, it was messy—and Coral Haven had been picking at the fallout ever since.

At first, Bauer stayed in the business. Quietly. A silent partner, if you will. His name was still on some of the paperwork. He'd stop by the store after hours, claim inventory; they'd argue in whispers behind the counter while Liz guzzled down wine to cope. Bauer's the type of guy who grew up around the tide. Steady, slow to anger, allergic to drama. When they split, he didn't hate her. Bauer wanted it to stay civil, maybe even friendly. He thought they could "just part ways and move on." Bauer presumed they could sign the papers, divide the business, and still nod at each other across Beach Street without the whole town whispering.

But then, something changed . . . Something switched in him. That easygoing, calm Bauer? It started to peel. What had been "amicable" turned into resentment. We all saw it clearly developing before our very eyes. It seeped out through avoidance, sarcasm, and anger that simmered just below the surface. He was still "zen" on the outside, but you could see the muscles in his forehead twitch when someone mentioned Liz's name.

By January, he was gone. By April, he had secretly leased the vacant storefront three doors down.

And right as summer season started, he had a new shop, a new sign, and a new blond girlfriend arranging outrageously expensive candles and freshly pressed coastal garments in the window.

*

I never really knew Bauer and Liz back when they were a "we." I only became invested in the aftermath; everyone loves a good tragedy. The stiff nods when they passed each other in town. The passive-aggressive digs in conversation. The way Liz never said Bauer's name, only *he* or *you know who* or just a tight-lipped look like someone had poured vinegar down her throat.

But I've lived long enough to know when something runs deep.

And this? This wasn't just heartbreak. It was betrayal with a business license.

The Sand Dollar had always felt like hers. But lately, when I walked by, I noticed the change. How much effort she was putting into the front displays, how speedily she replaced stock, how captivating her Facebook captions had gotten.

The store had gone from a boutique to a battlefield—a war zone with pretty lights and scented candles.

But there was something else. Something I hadn't noticed until today. When I passed by his new shop and saw him laughing with Ava on the porch, he seemed genuine, relaxed, like someone starting fresh. But I could tell that behind Bauer's smiling eyes there was a glint of anger . . . and guilt.

FIVE

It was a slow afternoon at The Driftwood. A muggy June day when even the seagulls couldn't be bothered to scream. The air was humid enough to drink, and everyone who came in looked like they'd been fighting the heat since sunrise. I spent most of my shift dealing with sunburned vacationers who barked orders like they were paying for a show, and college crews who thought endless mimosas made them enticing and confident. (They didn't).

The Driftwood was Coral Haven's tourist magnet, the place everyone hit once before heading home to brag about it. Tips were ridiculous during the season, so good that it almost made putting up with everyone's nonsense worth it. Almost. If I played it right, I could take the winter off, pay my bills, and still have money left over for the bar tab I swore I'd stop running up.

The place sat right across from the beach, in what used to be a Victorian hotel before someone decided to blow out the first floor and turn it into an open-air restaurant. Now it was all salt-stained charm and real driftwood. Driftwood on the walls, driftwood benches, driftwood bar. Driftwood toilets. If you could glue it to the surface, it probably had driftwood on it.

My coworkers were the real deal, though. Half locals who'd been here forever, half Europeans with a visa and accents that made the tourists tip better. Everyone was loyal to the owners, or at least loyal to the paycheck. We could squeeze in about two hundred people when it got busy, and we ran from nine a.m. to midnight. Our days had long, annoying, sticky shifts that ended with you smelling like fryer grease and burnt hot dogs. People sucked, sure. But when that stack of cash hit your apron at the end of the night, it was hard to complain too much.

*

I had a babysitting shift that evening, so I left The Driftwood a little early and took the main way home. Strolling the boardwalk past Beach Street, I used the time to reply to some text messages and to catch up on the local news and town happenings.

As I looked up from my flip phone, I noticed that the shop traffic was thinning out with the heat. A few tourists drifted between storefronts, holding ice cream and wide-brimmed beach hats they didn't know how to wear properly. I passed The Sand Dollar—the windows cleanly gleamed, and Liz had added a new sign out front:

Curated with soul, not spreadsheets.

I snorted under my breath, knowing exactly what she meant. Subtle . . . as always.

Then I kept walking. Three doors down, Bauer and Ava's newly named storefront, The Shore Thing (awfully similar), had its porch door propped open. The music had been turned off. The "Grand Opening" balloons were drooping a little, rubber tired from the heat.

I don't know why I paused. Curiosity got the best of me. As it got the best of everyone in town.

Maybe it was the way Bauer was standing near the counter, back turned, voice low, providing a steady presence. Maybe it was the fact that Ava's laugh sounded different, not bubbly like earlier, but clipped. Forced. Almost mean.

I stopped near the open porch window, hidden behind a rack of display towels fluttering in the breeze. I absolutely looked like a nosy creep.

"I just don't get it, hon. We tried to be civil with her," Ava was saying. "Enough is enough. She really thinks she can keep the place running without you this season? That store *was* you."

Bauer sighed. "It's pride. She won't let it go. She still thinks I'm going to come back and fix it all."

"She doesn't get to have it both ways, Bauer," Ava said. Her voice was lower now. "She ended things. You left. She made her bed. And now she gets to watch us build something better."

There was a brief silence.

Then Bauer said, "Babe, don't worry. She's not going to last. She doesn't know how much of that place I handled. Inventory, vendors, accounts . . . give it a month. Two. And she'll either sell or crash."

Ava stepped closer. "She won't have to worry much longer. Once this place takes off, she'll be done. I bet she'll leave town once her store closes."

Something in the way she said it made my skin go cold. It was casual, like she was talking about a clearance sale or an old shirt. Not a person.

Bauer didn't respond. He just looked down at his POS system.

Ava interjected herself into Bauer's silent thoughts. "I'm so proud of what we built together, babes. Let's not ruin it."

I backed away slowly, quietly.

Maybe it was just bitterness. A bad breakup, ugly words, nothing more.

But something about it seemed off.

It wasn't what they said. It was how they said it. Like Liz was already done. Like they were just waiting for the rest of the town to realize it.

*

This Week on the Dunes: Coral Haven Spout Off

Here's what everyone's been whispering about between sips of iced coffee and sandy strolls this week.

A Scoop Above the Rest?

Twisted Waves Ice Cream rolled out four brand-new summer flavors. Saturday's line stretched out the door and halfway down Beach Street as people couldn't wait to try Coconut Lime Swirl, Salted Caramel Crunch, Blueberry Cheesecake, and Chocolate Marshmallow Fudge. Early reviews? Coconut Lime Swirl might just be the flavor of the season. But don't take my word for it—go taste for yourself before the weekend rush.

Classrooms Getting Ready to Grow

Beachside Elementary has officially posted two open teaching positions for the fall. With more young families settling in Coral Haven (have you seen all the strollers on Morning Tide Lane lately?), the school is preparing for fuller classrooms and fresh faces. Interested applicants are encouraged to get their résumés in soon—the buzz is the spots will fill fast.

Parking Problems or Just Progress?

Seaside Square's seasonal overflow parking lot is open and ready for beachgoers—but not without a little muttering from the locals. Word on the street is that parking rates have quietly jumped this season, and not everyone's thrilled about the surprise price hike. A quiet grumble here, a side-eye there. Will this become a bigger town squabble? We'll keep an ear out.

Shop Talk—And Maybe a Little Tension?

Biggest news on Beach Street: Bauer Clips is setting up shop. His new place, The Shore Thing, opened its doors—and word is it's reminiscent of Liz Carper's long-loved Sand Dollar. Lovers turned business rivals? Maybe. Folks have already noticed some tense smiles and frosty nods when paths have crossed. Is Coral Haven in for a friendly competition . . . or something a little spicier?

That's the buzz for this week. Keep your shades on, your ears open, and your toes in the sand. See you on the dunes next week.

—Claire Bear

SIX

The Schmidt twins had somehow negotiated shared custody of their collectible U2 iPod without declaring war, and their dog, Wiley, limited herself to stealing just one slice of pizza. An act of restraint that felt worthy of a parade.

I reheated leftover slices, loaded the dishwasher, and spent an hour reading the same bedtime book three times because "my monster voice was funny." As I read the twins their bedtime stories, my mind was automatically making mental hints and ideas for my own stories.

By eight thirty, the house was quiet, the twins sound asleep. I pocketed the cash the parents handed over once they returned for the night and made my way out the door.

I wasn't planning to walk down Beach Street that evening, but I ended a bit early, and the stars were too beautiful to waste.

I'd just passed Blue Bottle Art, lost in thought about jumping into sweatpants and watching some reality TV, when I saw them—the scorned lovers.

Liz and Bauer.

They were outside The Sand Dollar, near the side alleyway by the truck loading and UPS entrance, trying to be discreet. Liz had one hand on her hip, the other pointed at him sharply, accusing. Bauer's arms were folded tight across his chest, his jaw clenched. I ducked behind the corner of a concession stand just out of reflex. I didn't mean to eavesdrop. But then again, this town literally begs you to.

"You do NOT get to act like the victim," Liz snapped. "You made your decision, Bauer. That was your choice. Don't rewrite it now just because your new hobby shop is behind schedule."

"Are you serious? It's not a fucking hobby shop," he countered, furious. "It's what I *should've* built years ago, without you micromanaging every goddamned thing."

"Oh, I'm sorry," she said with sarcastic sweetness. "Was my taste getting in the way of your damn spreadsheets?"

He stepped closer. Not quite threatening, but close enough that her posture slightly shifted.

"You think you're untouchable because you've been here longer," Bauer said. "But this street doesn't owe you anything. Loyalties change."

Liz laughed. Short and bitter. "You're still so good at pretending you're the normal one."

"I'm not pretending I'm anything," he said tiredly. "I'm just done with this game . . . or whatever this is." He motioned his arms between them. "Good luck this summer."

She turned and walked back toward her shop, muttering a brash *fuck you*, heels striking the pavement loudly with each staccato step. Bauer didn't follow.

I waited a full sixty seconds after he left before I moved again.

The store went dark, lights quickly flickering off, and I walked home fast, arms swinging, the warm night suddenly feeling a little too chilly.

*

What I witnessed between Liz and Bauer didn't sit right with me. Not just the argument, but the heat and passion behind their words, the history you could feel pulsing between every bitter sentence. That moment in the alleyway, something fractured. It wasn't just a fight between exes. There was hurt. Resentment. Power plays. And underneath all of it, a loss of unconditional love. Bauer's words, Liz's posture, the way neither of them lowered their voices. It all felt like a show meant to be heard, even if unintentionally. As I walked home, heart racing, I knew without a doubt: Whatever this tension was between them wasn't over.

By the time I got home, the house was quiet and dim, just the way I liked it after a long day. I kicked off my sandals at the door, shooting them haphazardly toward the hallway, and I made a beeline for the bathroom. My reflection in the mirror looked about as tired as I felt. Mascara slightly smudged, a faint indentation on my cheek from where I'd leaned against my hand babysitting.

Makeup off. Teeth brushed. Retainer in. It wasn't glitzy, but there was something deeply comforting about the routine. I pulled my hair up into a wild messy bun, slipped into an oversized fly-fishing T-shirt I'd been given by my dad, and wiped down the kitchen counter out of habit. The last bit of structure before surrendering to the night.

I grabbed a blanket, curled up on the couch, and slipped on my glasses—functional, not fashionable—then turned on the TV. The glow of a low-budget dating show filled the room, all drama and bad decisions. It was perfect. No tense business owners. Just people pretending to fall in love on some tropical island.

I let my body sink into the cushions. It was just me, my retainer, and trash television. Bliss.

SEVEN

Carly, Madison, Olivia, and I had planned to go to the annual Strawberry Festival that morning. It was held at one of the big family farms about ten minutes off the island, a farm where you could taste sugar and freshly cut grass long before you found parking.

The whole farm was alive. A dozen vendors were set up in neat little rows beneath string lights, and tables overflowed with ruby-red berries in wicker baskets. There were jars of homemade jam and local honey, strawberry shortcakes piled high with whipped cream, and cocktails that tasted like summer in a glass. Someone was singing softly with a guitar near the picnic tables—an old folk song about the sea—and kids with sticky fingers darted around with strawberry face paint and flower crowns.

Carly perused the strawberries while Madison flirted with the guy pouring strawberry sangria. Olivia and I kept sneaking little samples of everything we could, laughing when the syrup dripped down our wrists.

"If I eat one more free sample, they're going to ask me to get off the premises," Olivia said, licking jam off her thumb.

"You're just mad because your teeth are red," Carly teased, holding up her phone to take a picture. "Smile, Liv—you look like a vampire who shops at Shop Rite."

Madison nearly snorted her drink. "What? I never get your metaphors, Carly. Speaking of vampires, the sangria guy keeps trying to refill mine and winking while getting me drunk. Do I look like I'm complaining? Happy SINGLE GIRL SUMMER!"

"You look like you're about to stalk that guy behind the kettle corn stand," I said.

"If he owns it, even better, and totally worth it," she grinned, swirling her cup.

Carly rolled her eyes and lifted a basket of the biggest strawberries I'd ever seen. "I'm going to make pie," she announced proudly.

"You don't even have a pie pan, and you melted most of your cooking tools . . ." Olivia said.

"Details," Carly said, waving her off. "I'll improvise."

"Translation," I said, "these are going to sit in the back of your fridge until next weekend, when they're science experiments."

"Art," Carly corrected, pretending to be offended. "Fermentation and mold are art."

We all burst out laughing, sticky-fingered.

*

Making friends as an adult was something no one really prepared you for. But somehow, in Coral Haven, it happened so naturally.

When I left the city, I wasn't sure it ever would. My ex, Deacon, got all the friends in the breakup, like getting the kids in a divorce. They were "his" people now, the dinner-party crowd, the rooftop-bar regulars, the group texts that kept going without me. Starting over meant more than finding a new apartment; it meant figuring out who I was without that orbit.

So, when Coral Haven started to feel like home and when people actually remembered my name, it felt really cool. I was becoming a familiar face in the community.

I met Carly first. She'd just opened her Pilates studio on the second floor of a beachside plaza, in between a skate shop and a tiny art gallery. I'd wandered in one morning determined to find something to settle the anxiety in me, something to get me back into shape after too many café shifts and too many hours hunched over a laptop trying to wrangle an adorable yet educational book idea.

Carly's studio felt like walking into a well-made safe space. All soft whites, lavender candles, and sun pouring in through wide windows. And Carly herself? Warm, confident, grounded. She had that steady, graceful energy of someone who could keep her cool even if the ceiling caved in. We got along right away.

It was in one of Carly's late-morning classes that I met Madison and Olivia.

Madison had just moved back to Coral Haven after accepting an offer from the town's small hospital, landing a dream ER nurse role with a lot of autonomy and a short walk to the beach. She was short, adorable, sharp-witted, and full of fire that made you want her on your side in a crisis. She introduced herself while we were all fumbling with resistance bands, cracking a joke about how she hadn't stretched since high school cheerleading.

Olivia was a nice balance. She was quieter, with a dry, witty sense of humor and a kindness that showed up in the way she listened. She had grown up here in town, left for college two hours away, and returned to teach math at the same high school she once went to. Her roots ran deep.

The four of us just clicked. It didn't matter about our small age gaps or different career paths. What started as post-class chats turned into Friday beach walks, bar crawls, wine and movie nights, and instant messages that never felt obligatory.

*

I'd been cooped up with wild children and waitressing all week, so when Carly texted that they were grabbing drinks at the Barefoot Bar, I didn't think twice. I was getting nowhere with today's writing workshop, the cursor blinking tauntingly at the top of a blank page. I slammed the laptop shut and jolted out of my computer chair.

The evening sky glowed in soft layers of lavender, tangerine, and blush pink. It was a summer dusk that looked hand-painted. We squeezed around a patio table with sticky plastic menus and mismatched chairs, everyone relaxed from the sun and sea air.

The conversation was already buzzing with energy when I arrived. Olivia and Madison were going back and forth in their usual playful banter, voices rising with exaggerated indignation and laughter as they debated whether Liz or Bauer had been the more dramatic one in their breakup. Madison waved her hands animatedly, insisting Bauer had tried to stay professional, while Carly scoffed, rolling her eyes and grinning.

Then Carly leaned forward with a smirk. "Okay, but you weren't here the day Liz Carper chucked a frickin' moped helmet at Bauer's face in the middle of Beach Street. Like, in front of a bunch of tourists."

Madison, scrunching her nose, gasped and leaned in. "You're lying. No way."

"She did," said Olivia, wide-eyed and laughing. "It missed, but still. Honestly, impressive throwing arm."

Amusement erupted around the table. I found myself smiling, the tension of the week momentarily slipping off my shoulders. These women—Carly, Madison, Olivia—were my people here. Supportive, spirited, and always ready to rally behind one another.

"I just don't understand why they didn't close The Sand Dollar when they split up," Madison said. "Like, wouldn't you just want a clean break? Wipe your hands and walk away?"

"She built that store just as much as he did she said," I claimed before I could help myself.

"She's not doing herself any favors keeping it open," Adam said, and that's when I heard him chime in for the first time—quiet most of the night, nursing a beer and sitting on a barstool behind us.

Adam and I met maybe three or four times before. He was friends with Carly, Madison, and Olivia. Adam was always friendly and polite. The kind of guy who listened more than he talked, and when he did speak up, it was usually a comical retort.

Now, though, he looked up and said, "It just feels . . . sad, doesn't it? Like, the more she hangs on, the more obvious it is that Bauer was the real reason that place had any success."

Everyone abruptly went quiet.

He smiled apologetically and added while chuckling, "I mean—no offense. I'm sure she's trying. But it's like . . . keeping an old surfboard after it's cracked. Sentimental, but not functional."

I took a sip of my drink. *Damn, that was a great analogy, Adam.* I suddenly was aware of how tightly I was holding the plastic cup. "Or maybe it just takes time to find your flow again," I said.

Adam didn't respond, just tapped the side of his glass and looked up at the bar ceiling.

The conversation shifted after that. Someone brought up Ava's aggressive promo flyers, and we were off again, trading rumors like kids with Pokémon cards.

But that comment stuck with me. The way he said *cracked surfboard*—like Liz was adrift at sea, clinging to something she thought would save her but would only fall to pieces as soon as the waves got rough.

*

This Week on the Dunes: Summer Buzz

What a week here in Coral Haven! The kind where everyone's got that summer sparkle in their eyes.

Coast Guard Graduation Week!
If you've been near the boardwalk lately, you've probably spotted the cadets doing their final runs in uniform (and yes, they still wave back when you cheer). They're officially graduating this week and finding out where they'll be stationed—some heading north to chilly Maine, others out west. Coral Haven's going to feel a lot quieter without them grabbing midnight pizza from Tony's or crowding The

Driftwood for happy hour. Wishing them all calm seas and good coffee wherever they end up.

Fire in the Next Town Over
Not-so-fun news: There was a barn fire in Maple Shore, just twenty minutes off the island. No injuries (thankfully!), but the barn's a total loss. It belonged to the family who runs the fall hayrides—such kind people. Our volunteer firefighters helped out, of course. Big love to them for keeping everyone safe.

Storm Watch (Kind Of?)
And yes, everyone's favorite summer tradition—the "maybe-it's-a-hurricane, maybe-it's-not" panic. Forecasts say it might brush past Coral Haven midweek, but if you've lived here for more than a season, you know how this goes: Everyone stocks up on batteries and wine, then we get an hour of sideways rain and a power flicker. Still—stay safe, charge your flashlights, and bring those porch plants inside just in case.

Strawberry Festival Recap!
The farm looked like something straight out of a postcard—tables overflowing with berries, local honey, jams, and enough strawberry shortcake to put anyone into a sugar coma. The live music, the cocktails, the aroma of fresh grass and sugar—it was the perfect summer day.

In Other News . . .
The shops downtown are buzzing with early season sales. The Sand Dollar just got a new shipment of coastal-smelling candles and shell jewelry (Liz always has the prettiest displays). But it's not just Liz making waves. Three doors down, The Shore Thing—yes, that Shore Thing with Bauer and Ava—is rolling out its first round of "signature summer collections." Word around Beach Street is that the inventory looks awfully familiar to anyone who's stepped foot in The Sand Dollar over the past few years. Coincidence? Maybe. Coastal inspiration travels fast in Coral Haven, after all.

Anyway, that's the latest from our little corner of the coast. Here's hoping the week ahead stays calm, the storm drifts east, and no one loses their beach umbrella to the wind.

See you around town,
—Claire Bear

EIGHT

The crowd formed at The Sand Dollar before the explanation did.

I was at the smoothie shop, waiting on my drink, when I noticed half the line turn their heads as if they were watching a street performance. I followed their gaze and spotted Liz standing just outside her door, sunglasses on with an expression like stone.

Ava Delaney was there too.

I'd only seen her in passing. With her glossy hair and enviable style, she always looked like she belonged in an ad campaign for *Elle* magazine. She was standing close, too close, her voice low but stiff. I stepped away from the counter, casually, like I was checking the sidewalk for something, and caught just enough. Another public confrontation was brewing. This was the most exciting this town had ever been.

"You're actually pathetic, Liz. Honestly."

Liz didn't recoil. "You're ridiculous. It looks like you're still spying on my products to steal and sell them."

Ava laughed, but there was no humor in it. "This whole thing—keeping the boutique open, pretending you're above it all—it's embarrassing. You're hanging on by threads and acting like you're a victim."

"Must be exhausting," Liz said calmly. "Dating a *man child* who spends half his time robbing someone else's ideas and dreams."

Ava took a step forward. "We don't need to copy anything. Bauer and I are building something *better* here. And guess what? It's working. People are already choosing our boutique. Our sales are skyrocketing, Liz."

Liz tilted her head. "Okay, then why the hell are you still standing on *my* doorstep, Ava?"

Ava looked like she wanted to straight slap her. Instead, she scoffed and turned on her heel, trucking past a stunned tourist who was in the wrong place at the wrong time and stormed down the sidewalk toward The Shore Thing.

Liz watched her go the whole way, then exhaled slowly and went back inside, and I could see her already opening a bottle of wine.

The crowd dispersed as quickly as it formed. My smoothie was ready. But I couldn't rid the image of Ava's face—the tension in her jaw, the way her eyes flicked to the window like she wanted to smash it just to prove a point.

For a minute, it really did look like she hated Liz.

*

I was walking toward The Sand Dollar to check on Liz after the spicy confrontation when a shadow fell over the boardwalk planks in front of me.

"Claire."

The sound of my name stopped me cold.

Bauer Clips stood ten feet away, blocking the sunlight like some human wall. He wasn't smiling. His sunglasses hung from the heavy collar of his shirt, his jawline clenched, a vein visible near his temple. He moved toward me with slow, deliberate strides that made you realize just how broad he really was.

"I need a word," he said. Not a question, an order.

"Sure," I said carefully, forcing casual. "Everything okay?"

His laugh was short, bitter. "No, actually. Everything's not okay."

He stopped close enough that I could see the faint freckles dotting his cheeks, the faded lines bracketing his mouth. His elevens prominent. "You think I don't read that blog of yours? The one where you turn everyone's business into horseshit?"

My stomach twisted. "It's not—"

"Don't," he cut me off, his voice low and edged. "Don't spin it. You've been writing about me and Ava since the day we announced our new boutique. Half-truths and juvenile rumors dressed up as entertainment. You think it's harmless gossip? It's not. It's defamation."

My throat went dry. "I write what people talk about, what they're interested in. It's a community update, not—"

He took another slow step forward, closing the space between us until I could smell cedar from his aftershave. His eyes were pale, cold, and unblinking.

"You don't live here, not really," he said. "You're a loser, Claire. A fake local with a blog and too much time. And you're messing with my business."

I swallowed hard, speechless. Managing to squeak, "Bauer, it's not personal—"

"It is to me." His tone deepened. "You want to write about fresh pies and fireworks? Fine. But you mention my name or my Ava's again, and I swear to God, I'll drag you into court so fast you won't know what hit you, Claire. Defamation, invasion of privacy, whatever it takes. You'll lose your apartment, your job, your reputation. Everything. Have fun living in a town that despises you."

He leaned closer, lowering his voice until it barely carried above the daily humdrum. "You think I won't do it? Try me."

The breeze picked up, snapping a paper sign loose behind him. It flittered down the street. My pulse was piercing in my ears.

"You're threatening me?" I said. My voice quivered.

He smiled with his mouth strained and teeth showing. "No. I'm protecting what's mine."

He straightened, towering over me, eyes narrowing in that slow, assessing way that made my stomach turn. "You have no idea how hard I've worked for that shop. How much I've put into it. And I'm not about to let some washed-up wannabe writer ruin it because she needs something to chatter about."

The words hit harder than I expected. *Washed-up. Wannabe.*

"You should leave town," he added flatly. "Go back to wherever you came from. This place isn't for people like you."

He didn't wait for a response. He turned and walked away, shoulders tense, jaw set, his reflection warping in the shop windows as he passed.

As he strutted away, I just stared at him, replaying every word, every look, every inch of that anger he'd kept so carefully leashed. I'd never seen him like that.

And yet . . . beneath the fear, something else flickered—something stubborn, a fire.

I told myself he was just stressed. Under pressure. Trying to protect his business and his pride. This was Bauer's way of posturing power and lashing out at the nearest, closest target. It didn't make it right, but it made it . . . explainable.

I took a long breath and lifted my chin.

He didn't get to scare me into silence, into submission.

Writing was the only thing that had ever felt like mine. It was my therapy, my outlet, my way of understanding the world. I'd already lost one life back in the city; I wasn't about to let some overgrown bully take this one too.

When I got home, the adrenaline had cooled into something steadier: resolve. I opened my laptop, the screen lighting up my face, and pulled up my draft for next week's post. I wasn't stopping, and Bauer fuckface could eat it.

*

This Week on the Dunes: Salty, Sour, and Sweet

Maybe it's the humidity, or maybe everyone's just been spending too much time in each other's business (guilty), but Coral Haven feels a little . . . tense this week. The tension that makes people talk softer in public but type faster online.

A Wrinkle in the Retail Space?

Our local boutiques, for example, are giving the rest of us a master class in "friendly competition." Display windows are getting updated almost daily, prices are mysteriously dropping or rising depending on who you ask, and let's just say a few "coincidental" restocks have started more conversations. I'm sure it's all perfectly normal: creative minds, small-town energy, salt air. But something about it feels just a touch sharper than usual. Maybe it's just the summer rush setting in. Maybe everyone's just tired. (Or maybe there's only room for one queen of coastal chic. Who knows?)

Save Our Nature Preserves

Meanwhile, the Nature Preserve is launching its new guided sunset tours this weekend! They'll be taking groups along the marsh trail at low tide, pointing out herons, sandpipers, crabs, and all the creatures that come alive once the beach crowds clear out. The first tour filled up in under an hour, so if you're interested, get your name on the list early!

Hasta La Vista, Harvey's Shoes

And in other local news, we're saying goodbye to a longtime favorite: Harvey's Shoe & Surf is closing after nearly thirty years. Harvey's hanging up his laces (literally) to retire upstate near his grandkids. The store's been a fixture here for as long as most of us can remember, and it's going to feel strange walking past that empty window.

The season always brings a little extra drama along with the sunshine.
—Claire Bear

NINE

I turned down my comforter, fluffed my favorite pillow, and dimmed the little lamp on my nightstand until the room glowed soft and golden. I took two melatonin gummies, of course cherry flavor, and told myself I'd finally get a full night's sleep. No internet, no overthinking, no worrying.

I crawled into bed and pulled the blanket tight around my shoulders, letting the small sound of the ceiling fan drown out the rest of the world. My body was tired, but my mind wasn't listening. Every time I closed my eyes, I saw Bauer's face: tight-lipped, icy-eyed. The way his voice had cracked on the word *mine*. The cold, almost triumphant look when he warned me to stop writing. His anger clung to me.

Eventually, mental exhaustion won. But when I finally drifted off, it wasn't rest that found me.

I was back on Beach Street, but it didn't look right. The sky was bruised purple, the shop lights fluorescent and flickering like a cliché horror movie. The Sand Dollar's door was wide open, its wind chimes clattering minor keys in the dark.

Inside, I saw Liz. She was standing behind the counter, next to a broken wine glass, her hands trembling, bleeding where shards of glass punctured her skin, her eyes wide with a kind of terror that didn't belong on her face. Bauer was there too. His shirt was half unbuttoned, chest pouring blood, and his shadow spilled across the floor like oil.

"Bauer, stop. PLEASE," Liz said, voice breaking, body trembling.

But he didn't stop. His hand shot out, fast and brutal, forcefully gripping her by the wrist. I tried to move, to scream, but my feet wouldn't work. It was like I was stuck in quicksand, sinking with every heartbeat.

There was a violent, bone-smashing crunch and then she limply fell. A frightening sound, boom, whack, wood against wood. She started seizing and vomiting as her pulse slowly stopped. The shop went silent except for the creak of the door swinging in the wind.

Bauer turned. Slowly. His bloodshot eyes found me across the room. He was pale and wild, his mouth curling into something that wasn't quite a smile, more of a foaming sneer.

"See what you did, bitch? See what you made me do?" he said.

I ran, or tried to with all my might, but I wasn't moving forward. My lungs burned, my legs heavy as if

Bauer himself were holding me back, as if he'd sunk his fingernails into my skin. His footsteps thundered behind me, closer, faster, until I could feel his hot breath at my neck . . .

I woke up gasping.

My sheets were twisted, damp with sweat, my heart punching against my ribs. For half a second, I couldn't tell what was real—the sound of waves outside my window or the echo of his footsteps still chasing me.

It was just a dream, I told myself. *Just a dream.*

I lay there until sunrise, watching the ceiling blush pink with the first light, trying to shake the feeling that the dream was random, that my subconscious wasn't trying to tell me something.

By morning, I knew I needed to get out of Coral Haven. Just for a hot sec.

*

The drive back to my parents' house only took a couple hours, but it felt like I'd crossed into another universe. No boardwalk, no gossiping neighbors, no whispers about broken hearts or candle shop rivalries. Just the quiet buzz of cicadas and the familiar comfort of my childhood street.

An hour into my drive, I ended up behind the world's slowest driver. The kind who clearly believes the speed limit was more of a *polite suggestion*. I beeped once, twice, three times, tried to stay patient, didn't, and started flicking my high beams on and off, but they *still* wouldn't move. I gave them a dramatic thumbs-down as I passed them. Petty, yes. Satisfying? Absolutely.

When I finally turned into my parents' neighborhood, everything felt smaller and quieter, softer around the edges. Their house sat halfway down the block. A cheerful split-level painted a buttery yellow with a pale blue roof that always reminded me of summer skies.

Mom's garden had exploded since the last time I was home: hydrangeas in full bloom, daisies spilling over the walkway, and tomato plants standing tall like proud little soldiers. She'd turned landscaping into a full-time passion project years ago, and it showed.

She could never leave anything exactly as it was, not the garden, not the furniture, not even the rocks bordering the flower beds. Every visit felt like walking into a slightly new version of the same home. Pots rearranged, colors shifted, something freshly painted or restyled. The decor was always a surprise, and one that somehow made the house feel even more alive.

Mom was already at the door when I pulled up, apron dusted with flour. Dad followed, grinning like I'd been gone for months instead of weeks.

"Claire Bear!" he said, pulling me into a hug that smelled like aftershave and barbecue smoke.

Dinner was waiting: grilled chicken, roasted potatoes, green beans slicked with butter. A meal that wrapped itself around you like a warm blanket. We sat at the kitchen table, the one with faint scratches and dents from my high school homework marathons. Mom peppered me with questions before I'd even cut into my food.

"So, how's the café? Your writing? Your friends? Any news from that little town of yours?"

I speared a green bean. "Well, there's been some interesting fuss." I eagerly continued, "Liz Carper, the one who owns The Sand Dollar? She and Bauer Clips, her ex-fiancé, had a real shitty falling-out over money. And now he's with this girl Ava, who isn't exactly winning the town popularity contest. She's kinda like an ice-cold bitch."

Mom raised her eyebrows. "Language, Claire. That's some drama alright! But honey, I don't remember these names. Am I supposed to? Carpet and Soup are fighting over what?"

Dad chuckled, shaking his head. "Ignore your mom. Small towns. Nothing ever stays quiet. That sounds very interesting, Claire."

"Oh well. They're fine, though?" Mom asked, and again. "Your friends?"

"Yeah. Carly, Madison, Olivia. They're good. Busy, but good. They've basically adopted me at this point."

Mom smiled at that, her eyes warm. "I'm glad you've found some really good people, Claire Bear. It's truly wonderful!"

Dad carved into the chicken like it was a full-on cooking show for us. "Well," he said, "I officially turned in my keycard today."

Mom clasped her hands together. "He's a retired man now. Isn't that just wild, Claire? No more alarm clocks. You wouldn't believe how happy he wakes up!"

I grinned. "That's huge! So, what's the plan, Dad? Gonna build fishing rods or drive Mom batshit crazy full-time?"

He laughed, the sound deep and proud. "A little of both, probably. But we've been talking. We're doing an Alaskan cruise in July with your aunt and uncle, then maybe some island-hopping in Hawaii. Your mom's already bought ten different orthopedic sneakers."

Mom rolled her eyes affectionately. "It's a big world, and we've been stuck in the same ZIP code for thirty-some years. It's about time we go somewhere that doesn't serve clam chowder as the house special."

I smiled, stabbing a piece of dark meat. "I'm so excited for you guys. Really. You deserve it. Take so many photos! We can look at them together, when you're back."

Mom reached for her wine glass, her expression softening. "That's the plan, sweetheart. You've been working hard too! You should take a vacation one of these days. Maybe join us somewhere."

"Tempting," I said, smiling into my plate. "But I need to work to make money to live in society. I think town might be enough change and adventure for me right now."

Dad chuckled. "As long as you're happy, kiddo. That's all that matters. We love you, Claire."

*

After dinner, I walked into my old bedroom. It was like stepping into a time capsule that never quite got sealed shut. The walls were still the same soft gray my mom painted when I was fifteen—"calming," she'd called it—though a few scuff marks, dings from secret drunken sleepovers, and thumbtack holes betrayed my teenage restlessness. The queen bed sat in the corner, topped with the comforter Mom had made using my old soccer T-shirts, each stitched square a different shade of nostalgia. It was lumpy in spots, but it was home.

Magazine cutouts of Jesse McCartney, Adam Brody, and Johnny Depp plastered the walls, a trifecta of crushes that said way too much about who I was as a girl. The carpet was still the same pale beige, now stained near the dresser from that one time I tried to dye my hair "black" and ended up with purple streaks and a permanent reminder of my teenage rebellion.

Mom fussed about whether I had enough groceries, Dad tried to slip me gas money, and I let myself sink into the rhythm of being their daughter again instead of Coral Haven's amateur gossip correspondent.

I loaded Candy, my silver Honda Civic that had seen better decades but still refused to die. She'd rolled past the hundred-thousand-mile mark ages ago, and I swear she groaned every time I asked her to start. Three of her four windows still worked automatically, the fourth needed a little persuasion and a strong elbow. Candy had character, loyalty, and just enough quirks to match mine. She'd been with me through cross-town heartbreaks, job changes, and one very questionable camping phase.

The air-conditioning wheezed to life as I pulled out of the driveway, the highway stretched ahead of me.

After that nightmare about Bauer and Liz, being home felt like therapy I didn't know I needed. There weren't any crime scenes, incessant gossip, or white shop lights haunting my dreams, just the quiet reassurance of people who loved me without question.

With the windows cracked and the breeze sneaking back in, I actually felt hopeful that tensions would cool around town. Maybe that dream had been my brain's way of purging the stress, shaking loose the fear that had burrowed in since that confrontation.

The *Welcome to Coral Haven* sign glowed in the dusk. I exhaled, telling myself that tonight, I'd sleep without ghosts scratching at my dreams.

I had no idea the town would wake to its own nightmare.

That by morning, Liz Carper would be found dead.

No one in Coral Haven heard a cry for help.
The waves kept rolling. The gulls kept circling.

TEN

By the time someone screamed, it was already too late.

Coral Haven had stopped moving.

The morning Liz was found dead, the air buzzed like a power line. The atmosphere too flashy, too stagnant, and impossible to ignore. The news rippled through town like a shockwave, each retelling jagged and breathless.

I was slowly beginning a shift at The Driftwood, balancing a tray of coffee mugs while the crowd thinned and thickened in uneven waves. Conversations dropped off mid-sentence. A couple at the counter leaned closer together, faces pinched. Someone gasped near the hostess stand. No one laughed.

My pink Razr buzzed in the pocket of my apron.

Carly: *OMG police at shops. Ambulances?*

My stomach flipped. I didn't even bother answering. My texting plan was already shot for the month.

I chucked the coffee tray down on the nearest counter, untied my apron, and grabbed my sunglasses without so much as looking for my manager. I was out the door before anyone could stop me, the bell above it ringing too cheerfully as I stepped into the street.

News doesn't travel here; it detonates. By eight a.m., the coffee shop crowd was whispering, phones pressed to their ears, eyes wide and wet. By eight thirty, the local radio station had cut into the morning playlist. By nine, there was a very active crime scene.

When I reached Beach Street, the sight hit me square in the chest. Yellow tape stretched across the entrance of The Sand Dollar, snapping in the wind like a cruel party streamer. The cheerful window displays filled with hand-painted jewelry, sun-bleached starfish, and bright custom artwork looked grotesque behind the cordon, mocking in their normalcy. Two officers stood rigid at the doorway, arms crossed, faces carved into stone. You could tell from the way they avoided each other's eyes that whatever they'd seen inside wasn't leaving them anytime soon.

The crowd along the sidewalk whined, fragmented whispers colliding midair.

"Someone found her inside," a woman grumbled to her friend, clutching a coffee cup with both hands.

"Inside?" the other echoed.

The first nodded. "Yeah, they said it's bad. Blood! Everywhere. Fire department was called to ventilate the smoke. God, I think she's dead."

I froze. Dead? I didn't see smoke—or smell it. I figured the rumors were already getting out of hand.

"Claire!" a distant voice called.

I turned to see Carly jogging toward me, her ponytail swinging, yoga mat slung over one shoulder. Her face was pale beneath her sun-kissed skin.

"Oh my God, what the hell is happening?" she asked, breathless. "I heard sirens and saw all the tape."

"I don't know," I said quickly, my throat dry. "Carly, it's Liz's store. They said someone found her this morning. I think it's bad. Really bad."

Carly's hand flew to her mouth. "No way. *Liz?*" Her voice cracked. She took a shaky step closer to the curb, her eyes darting between the officers and the shuttered door. "I just saw her two days ago when I stopped in to grab that new diffuser. She seemed like, fine. Pissed off, but fine."

"I know." I swallowed hard. "They're saying someone found her—like, found her *inside*."

The words came out thinner than I meant them to.

Carly blinked fast, her eyes glassy. "Holy shit."

We stood shoulder to shoulder, the two of us silent among the whispers rising from the crowd. It felt like the whole town had migrated here. The locals and tourists lingering too long, kids tugging at their parents' sleeves, everyone waiting with bated breath. No one admitted they were staring, but no one looked away.

Across the street, I caught sight of The Shore Thing. Its front windows were dark, but a strip of display lighting inside still glowed, throwing the interior into sharp focus. The light hit Bauer like a spotlight, giving me a clear, uninterrupted sightline through the glass.

He was pacing, phone pressed to his ear, eyes sharp, his hand dragging over his mouth again and again. From here, he looked hollow—drained of color, eyelids swollen. If he was faking shock, he deserved an Oscar.

Carly followed my gaze. "Is that Bauer?" she whispered.

"Yeah."

"God, that's . . . that's . . ." she said, shaking her head. Then she glanced at her watch, face twisting with an unreadable emotion. "I've got a Pilates class in ten minutes. I can't even cancel it. It's full, and the studio's expecting me."

"It's okay. Go. I'll stay. Someone needs to . . . I don't know. Just . . . see what's happening," I said.

Carly hesitated. "Promise you'll text me the second you find out something?"

"I will." Still pissed off about my phone's texting plan.

She squeezed my arm, her fingers cold despite the rising sun. "Talk soon, babe, okay?"

Then she jogged off down the street, the strap of her mat bouncing against her back, vanishing into the swirl of voices and flashing lights.

I turned back to The Sand Dollar.

Rumors leaked in fragments, carried from lip to lip. Somewhat like a game of whisper down the lane.

It was a runner who found her. A woman Liz knew well enough to wave to, to chat with in passing, but not well enough to call a close friend. From what I could gather, she was halfway through her usual morning route when she noticed the lights on inside The Sand Dollar, bright and unmistakable against the quiet street.

It struck her as odd. Liz was notorious about the electric bill, always complaining about it, always double-checking switches before locking up for the night. Still, the runner told herself it was nothing. Maybe Liz had come in early. Maybe she'd forgotten to turn them off.

The runner figured she'd just pop in to say hi. The front door was unlocked.

That didn't phase her, not at first. Liz forgot things sometimes. Keys, receipts, the occasional lock. The runner pushed the door open, called out her name once, then again.

And then she saw her.

Not standing. Not even slumped. Just . . . gone. Her body stiff, twisted in an awful angle that didn't look human anymore. Someone whispered there'd been vomit pooled on the hardwood, streaked and sour, the unmistakable sign of a body shutting itself down. Another voice added that her eyes were open. Staring. Fixed.

A ripple of silence spread through the crowd when two officers emerged from the shop, their faces pale and drawn. One of them spoke low to the other, but his voice carried just enough for those of us closest to hear.

"She's gone, no pulse," he said grimly. "Call the county. We'll need the medical examiner."

The words landed like stones. *She's gone.* The whispers had turned into fact.

The dread settled like damp into the bones of Coral Haven.

A few storefronts down, Adam stood with a small group of people, his hands shoved deep in his pockets, his face unreadable. He looked like he was watching a performance—detached, still. His eyes wandered until they lay on Bauer.

And me? I couldn't move. My feet felt rooted to the pavement, my gaze locked on the door I'd walked through a hundred times. The same door Liz had propped open on stale afternoons, the same counter where she'd lived and laughed . . . and loved.

Now it was sealed behind tape and silence.

Liz Carper was very dead.

ELEVEN

Beach Street was ablaze with flashing red and blue lights of five police cars, harsh colors that made everything look wrong. Familiar storefronts wore ugly shadows that pulsed with every rotation of the sirens. The cheerful string lights that normally twinkled above the boardwalk now looked cruel, pale, fluorescent, anemic against the violence of the crime scene tape.

Bright yellow strips fluttered in the breeze, cutting across the entrance of The Sand Dollar like a warning no one could ignore. Officers paced with clipboards, radios crackling, voices low but urgent. The whole street smelled different too; the briny tang of the ocean carried something metallic, almost electric.

I pressed closer to the edge of the crowd, my stomach sinking, heart rate sky rocketing. The people around me, neighbors, shopkeepers, and tourists who'd wandered into something they didn't understand, spoke in whispers that seemed to dissolve into the air. No one said Liz's name. It was as though saying it out loud would summon something terrible.

Then the front doors opened.

Two paramedics wheeled a silver stretcher through the doorway. Atop it, zipped inside black plastic, lay the unmistakable shape of a body.

Liz.

I felt my knees go soft, my hands gripping the rail of the boardwalk for balance.

Just last week, I'd stood in Liz's shop while Carly wandered between the shelves, loading her arms with fresh candles for the Pilates studio.

"If you take Bauer and Ava to court," Carly said, squinting at a label, "I'll testify. I don't know what about, but I'm sure I can make something super evil up."

Liz snickered from behind the counter, shaking her head as she rang everything up. "If I end up fighting them in court, I swear it'll be over my dead body."

We laughed. None of us thought it would matter.

And now she was being rolled away like an object on a catering cart. Anonymous. Silent.

Gasps broke out in the crowd. A woman near me covered her mouth. A man muttered "Oh, God" into his hands, trying to not vomit. But mostly, there was silence. That terrible, reverent silence that felt stronger than any scream.

A woman in crisp, dark business attire with a shiny badge moved with calm authority through the swarm of uniforms. Her presence was like a blade slicing through fog—precise, steady, dangerous. She snapped her notebook shut and signaled to the coroner's van.

"Get her to the medical examiner. Hey, use gloves! Don't contaminate the possible crime scene, Jesus Christ. The cause of death needs confirmation. No assumptions," she barked, her voice brisk and certain. "We work with facts. God, these morons."

The van doors slammed shut. The engine roared to life. I flinched at the sound.

"Has the body been officially identified?" she asked a nearby officer.

"Not officially, however strong speculation it is Elizabeth," he replied.

"Okay, work on that. Good. Notify next of kin. Collect statements. No speculation until we have clarity."

Her commands came fast. This wasn't her first rodeo.

"Full sweep," she told the CSI team when they arrived. "Every surface, every counter, every object. Fingerprints, trace evidence, I don't care if it's a speck of dust. I want it catalogued. Get security footage from every shop on this block. We need to know every person who crossed this street today."

Another investigator emerged from the shop, holding an evidence bag. Inside was something small, shimmery, glinting a shade of silver faintly beneath the overhead lights.

"Found this. Possible clue. No visible prints."

"Bag it and log it," the female detective said. "Analysis back at the station."

Her face betrayed nothing. No fear. Just hard lines. She turned toward the crowd for a moment, eyes sweeping over us, and the way her gaze cut through made my pulse quicken.

"We're going to figure out what happened here. Not a single detail gets missed, we do this by the book. Clear?"

The words hung in the night.

That was when it hit me. Coral Haven wasn't the same place I'd driven home a mere sixteen hours ago. Whatever innocence lingered on these streets had been zipped into that black bag and wheeled away.

This wasn't drama. This wasn't gossip.

This was possible murder.

And in a town this small, it meant one thing: The killer was standing among us.

TWELVE

Even standing still made my skin damp, my armpits slick with sweat.

I was still wearing my work uniform, the fabric clinging to me like glue, heavy and uncomfortable in the humidity. I could smell coffee on my skin, and my hands felt faintly sticky, like I hadn't quite managed to wash the shift off yet.

After a few questions and some careful eavesdropping, I learned that the woman at the scene shouting orders would be leading the investigation, and her name was Detective Natalie Hensley.

She wasn't exactly what I'd expected from someone who'd seen too many sunbaked crime scenes. Long black hair slicked back into a precise bun, professional uniform crisp and pressed despite the heat, and light brown eyes that moved like searchlights, scanning over each person, catching every twitch, every whisper. She didn't look frazzled or hurried; she owned the ground beneath her boots.

Detective Hensley stood at the edge of the crime scene caution tape, her presence commanding without even raising her voice. "Everyone here will need to provide contact information," she announced, tone calm but cutting through the noise like a blade. "Officers will be taking names and statements. We'll be calling each of you to the station in the next few days for formal questioning. We need everyone's cooperation."

Low sounds ran through the small crowd, everyone uneasy. Locals fanned themselves with their hands and newspapers, kids clung to parents' legs, and the air filled with nervous energy. The officers moved with practiced tempo, clipboards, radios, calm urgency. The town hadn't seen this kind of commotion since Hurricane David volunteer cleanup years ago.

And then I heard someone behind me whisper, "Wait—Hensley? As in *that* Detective Hensley?"

A large woman in huge oval bifocals said toward the person next to her, "Yeah, she's the one from that murder-suicide case over in Willow Hawk last year. It was all over the papers."

Her friend's brows rose. "Oh my God, I remember that. They said she was the one who cracked it. The crazy husband who locked them in the car with the exhaust on? The big carbon monoxide story?"

"Yep. Tough as nails, apparently," the first woman said. Her face soured. "And kind of bitchy if you cross her."

The words carried just far enough for me to catch them. I couldn't help sneaking another look at Hensley. She didn't seem to hear the whispers, or maybe she just didn't care.

Her focus was absolute, scanning every face like a human lie detector. She barked an order to one of the younger officers, her tone curt but never cruel.

For some reason, that fascinated me. She wasn't the type who got lost in small-town gossip or swayed by sentiment, like me. She looked like someone who'd seen what real monsters were made of and still managed to keep her uniform pressed.

Then, the realization hit me like a small jolt of electricity. Whatever happened to Liz Carper was big enough to draw *her*.

*

Detective Hensley stood near The Sand Dollar's entrance, her posture straight and deliberate, scanning faces like she was mentally arranging them on a chessboard. She turned to one of the officers beside her.

"Questioning. Start with anyone who owns property on this block and move outward," she said. "We're building a timeline."

The officer nodded and hurried off, blindly following her instructions. Respect. Hensley's gaze swept across the street again, sharp and assessing, until it landed on me.

"Ms. Collins, correct?" she called out.

I blinked. *Uh, what?* Hearing my name in that clipped, authoritative voice startled me. "Yes?"

A trace of recognition crossed her face. Not surprised, exactly, more like confirmation.

"I thought so. I've seen your face before," she said, stepping closer. "You write and run that local blog, don't you? *The Dune Diaries.* You keep a close eye on this town."

"It's *This Week on the Dunes*," I corrected automatically, then immediately regretted the counter. "But yes. That's me."

She gave a small, decisive nod. "Good. Thought so. I'd like to ask you a few questions now, if you don't mind."

Around us, officers were starting to usher small groups toward patrol cars and benches. You could feel the unease spreading like fog. A young server from The Driftwood was crying softly near the coffee shop, mascara pooling under her eyes.

Detective Hensley gestured for me to follow. False guilt gnawed at me even though I knew I hadn't done anything. We walked a short distance to the police station near the boardwalk. A squat brick building wedged between town hall and the post office—historical, of course.

The transition from the briny, moist outside air to the chill of the AC was like being dunked in cold water. Inside smelled faintly of burnt coffee and dusty paper, the scent of long hours and bad news.

She offered me a bottle of water, which I declined, mostly because my throat was too clenched to swallow.

"Do you know why you're here, Ms. Collins?" she asked, voice level but probing.

I nodded slowly. "Yes, I'm guessing Liz Carper. I . . . heard what happened. Is it true, the rumors? Do you really think she was murdered?"

Her gaze narrowed and she dismissed my question. "All we know right now is that a woman is dead. Did you have anything to do with that??"

The interrogative examination hit harder than I expected. "Of course I didn't!" I practically yelled back. "Why would I? I liked Liz. Everyone liked Liz."

"You'd be surprised," Hensley said softly, jotting something in her notebook. "People hide resentment in strange ways. I need to cover all the bases and possibilities."

"I was at my parents' house last night," I blurted, trying to sound calm. "I left town yesterday afternoon. You can ask them."

She looked up, assessing me. "We will. You don't strike me as the type, Ms. Collins, but sometimes the type surprises me."

I swallowed, a bit skeptical. "I don't have a motive, if that's what you're implying."

She didn't respond, just flipped a page. "You recently saw Liz, right? You mentioned her in your blog. The new inventory, a positive write-up. A quip about Bauer and Ava. Were you friends?"

"Not friends exactly. A little more than acquaintances. Everyone kind of runs in the same circle here," I said, hearing my voice wobble. "I shopped at her store. We'd talk about business, books, gossip. The usual small-town stuff."

"And Bauer?"

"What about Bauer?" I asked.

Her pen hovered. "Do you know anything about him?"

"I met him before I even knew Liz," I said. "I'm sure you've heard, but they had a . . . complicated breakup. I've seen them argue. Publicly. Heard things too. About money. About Ava. That's all."

"Go on."

So I did.

I told her about the arguments. About Ava's coldness. And then—a memory suddenly surfacing—I told her about the way Liz had seemed lately.

A flash of the grocery store cut through me: Liz by the produce bins, shoulders drawn in tight, her body looking frail. The way her hands had trembled as she fumbled with her wallet. *Just tired,* she'd said. *Stomach's been off.*

"She looked worn down," I said now, choosing my words carefully. "Pale. Distracted. Like she was running herself ragged trying to keep up."

"She was scared of losing her business," I added. "Maybe her reputation. But not . . . not scared for her life."

Hensley's eyes flicked up. "Did she ever mention feeling threatened? By anyone?"

"No," I admitted. "But she did seem like something was eating at her."

I hesitated, then asked the question I hadn't meant to say out loud. "Do you think it was one of them?"

Her expression didn't change. "It's far too early to make assumptions, Ms. Collins. We're looking into all possible leads. Everyone is a suspect until we can prove otherwise."

Everyone. The word landed in my gut.

"Bauer was near the scene, wasn't he?" I asked, testing her reaction. "Don't killers usually hang around after they do it? To see the fallout? Haven't you seen *Dateline*?"

For a second, I thought I saw amusement washing over her eyes. "You're asking a lot of questions for someone who's supposed to be answering them."

I forced a thin smile. "Just a curious mind."

She closed her notebook. "We may have more to discuss later. Don't leave town."

"I live here full-time," I said, rising. "I'm not going anywhere."

Her gaze followed me to the door. "Good," she said. "Because I have a feeling you're going to be useful."

THIRTEEN

We walked the few blocks back together. I noticed there was no music spilling from shop doorways, no tourists laughing over street entertainers. Just the low whispers of neighbors gossiping in cliques, casting sneaky glances toward Bauer and Ava's boutique.

The Shore Thing was dark and empty. Closed. Only one sign hung neatly in the window: "Out of Office."

A police cruiser idled outside the store, the engine purring, while Detective Hensley and another officer made a beeline toward Bauer and Ava.

I paused across the street, pretending to check my phone but really watching them. I thought, *Maybe I should give them some privacy . . . Fuck it, this is way too good.*

Bauer fidgeted nervously, running a hand through his hair, his jaw clenched. Ava stood perfectly still, arms crossed, round-framed sunglasses hiding her eyes, her mouth a thin, hard line.

Detective Hensley was talking low, unsuccessfully trying to avoid the public overhearing their interaction. Then she gestured toward the car.

"We'll need you both to come to the county station for some questions," I heard her say. "We've got some details to sort out, alibis to confirm."

Bauer murmured something I couldn't catch. Ava turned her head toward him, lips moving fast. They looked like a couple on the verge of collapse, their bright, shiny store closed, their first season seemingly in ruins.

The police guided them into separate cruisers. Doors slammed. The police cars rumbled away down the block.

I stood there, heart tapping fast against my ribs.

If anyone on this street hated Liz Carper enough to kill her, it was Ava. I'd seen the look in her eyes that day outside The Sand Dollar. She radiated fury, pure and sharp. A grudge so big it felt like a dark shadow stretching over the town.

And now she and Bauer were the obvious prime suspects. The town would eat this up.

*

Feeling anxious, I met up with Madison, Carly, and Olivia at The Barefoot Bar . . . again.

We'd had the plan for weeks. Barefoot drinks had become our ritual, a way to unwind after long shifts, intense workouts, annoying, bratty summer school students, and chaotic medical emergencies (mainly removing objects shoved up a no-no zone). At first, I wasn't sure if it was appropriate to go out and have fun, not after what happened. Liz was dead. It felt wrong to even think about laughing or sipping a cocktail.

But the girls insisted and I couldn't say no. "It's better if we're together," Carly had said over the phone. "Safer in numbers. None of us should be alone tonight."

So I went.

When I walked in, they were already huddled in a booth, mid-conversation about the same thing on everyone's mind. The police interviews. Detective Hensley and her bandits had been making their rounds all day. Olivia said she'd been called to the local station that afternoon, asked the same sharp questions I'd been: where she was that morning, where she was last night, when she last saw Liz, whether she'd ever heard Liz and Bauer fight. What was her impression of Ava. Were they friends, did they hang out? Madison was next; she was pulled from her shift at the hospital for a "quick statement" that stretched nearly an hour long. Then Carly got questioned. They snagged her while she was locking up her studio, though she said Hensley's tone with her was almost friendly, like she was trying to read her without spooking her. We were all a little rattled, all quietly wondering if one of us had said the wrong thing. The four of us simultaneously took a large sip of our drinks.

Despite the newly ongoing tragedy, The Barefoot Bar was packed and the smell of stale beer and fried shrimp lingered. Locals huddled around the bar, talking in low, urgent voices. A cover band played upbeat rock music near the patio, but nobody was really listening. Every note seemed to fall flat against worry and glares around the room.

The bartenders were quieter than usual. There was no shouting over the music, no easy smiles. Only hasty movements and steady drink refills, their eyes widening toward the door every time it opened.

The crew next to us was getting quite rambunctious, so we found a nicer high-top table near the back. The table's lacquered wood felt sticky under my forearms. I traced the condensation ring from my glass just to keep my hands busy. A fidgeting habit.

"So, get this," Madison said, leaning in like she was about to spill a secret that would get her fired from a government job. "Apparently Liz owed Bauer ten grand. Like, since winter. For inventory or something, I don't know, from when they split The Sand Dollar."

"Seriously? How do you know this, Mads?" Carly frowned. "From what I heard, I thought they settled all that when he opened The Shore Thing."

Madison shook her head. "Nope. My cousin's friend works at the bank, she says Liz never paid him back. It was a big deal. Especially once Ava got involved, a.k.a. aggressively inserted herself into the situation. She was pushing Bauer to threaten legal action. Supposedly, she wanted the debt settled before their grand opening."

I swirled the ice in my drink, the cubes clinking against the glass. "They were still fighting about money. Even after they split and separated? Enough time had passed for Liz to pay."

"Totally," Olivia said. "Ava hated that Bauer let Liz get away with it for so long. She was trying to make him press harder. You know the vibe Ava gives, she's always the business shark."

"Sounds like a motive if you ask me," Carly said freely, finishing her drink accompanied by a large gulp.

The table went quiet for a moment. The music blurred into the background, some pop song about summer love that suddenly felt cruelly out of place.

I looked around the room. Every conversation seemed to circle back to the same thing. Liz, Bauer, Ava. The potential murder. The word still didn't feel real when I said it in my head.

The Barefoot Bar had always been our escape with dim lights, good music, excellent gossip. But tonight, it felt like a gathering of ghosts, everyone trying to make sense of what had just cracked open in Coral Haven.

I took a slow sip of my drink, the lime stinging my split lip. "It's going to be a long, weird summer," I said quietly.

Liv nodded. "Yeah. Totally feels like the kind that stains and changes everything. Coral Haven is first-page news. And that isn't always a good thing."

FOURTEEN

The weight of Liz's death hung over Beach Street, hauntingly.

At my shift, every customer who stepped into The Driftwood spoke in hushed tones, casting wary looks toward the door as if expecting news of an update at any moment, dramatic.

The place had filled with the usual mix of tipsy tourists and locals. A group of teenage surfers piled into a corner booth, their towels dripping onto the benches, the smell of saltwater following them in. They started off loud, bragging about the waves, laughing with that easy arrogance only seventeen-year-olds can pull off. But then the conversation shifted.

Liz's name slipped in, casual at first, then sharper. I caught fragments between orders. Words that twisted what had happened to her into something cheap and ugly. They joked about the paramedics. Said if Liz were still alive, she'd probably have fucked the one who carried her dead body out. They all laughed, that snickering, insensitive kind of laughter that's half evil and half thrill.

How disgusting. I scoffed and turned away, giving their table to a coworker.

*

Midway through my shift, while delivering sandwiches and iced teas to a family squished in a nearby booth, a quiet conversation caught my ear.

"—poison, they said. Can you believe it? Not a single cut or bruise. Just . . . poison."

I paused, pretending to adjust a napkin holder at the next table, straining to hear more.

"Antifreeze," the older woman whispered, leaning close to her friend. "That's what the toxicology report showed, I heard. There were traces on her hands too. And vomit near the body. The police are saying it could've been suicide." She rambled off, seeming too confident in her information. I was surprised to hear the word "toxicology" so quickly after Liz's death.

"Suicide? Liz?" Her friend scoffed, stirring the ice in her cup. "No way. She was too stubborn to go out like that. She was fighting her ex every step of the way, I heard. And her shop was doing fine, I think. There was always foot traffic. Oh, how awful!"

"That's what makes it strange. The police haven't ruled out murder, but . . . antifreeze . . . in her system? Like she willingly drank it herself?"

I moved past them quickly, trying to quiet the noise in my head. Suicide, antifreeze? Where were they hearing this? Liz never seemed like the type. Even on her worst days, she burned bright. Witty, fierce, determined when she spoke about her store and the future she wanted.

I dropped off a check at another table and ducked behind the counter, rearranging and sorting silverware while the low buzz of speculation swirled around the café.

"Maybe she poisoned herself by accident," someone murmured. "Or maybe someone made it look like suicide."

A shiver crawled down my spine. Liz, taking her own life? It didn't fit. The presence of a large quantity of antifreeze in her system. It seemed so chaotic and random. Possibly staged? My mind raced, turning over every detail I'd overheard, trying to piece together the facts. I wasn't going to let vicious rumors taint the truth of Liz's death.

I glanced toward the front window, my heart picking up speed as I spotted Bauer's boutique across the street. Still closed. The police tape stretched tight across The Sand Dollar, motionless in the afternoon light.

*

Later that night, I sat alone in my apartment with a cup of tea growing cold in my hands. The events of the past few days circled my mind like vultures. I began to summarize:

Liz and Bauer. They had been inseparable for years as childhood sweethearts who turned their love into a shared dream: The Sand Dollar. Then came the ugly split, the bitter divide of not just their relationship but their business. Liz got the shop. Bauer got the resentment and an unpaid settlement but found new love. And Ava, a brash and territorial woman, had leapt in to claim the space and boutique beside him. Replacing Liz as if trying to be a newer, better version.

It was hard to forget the very open and public arguments between Liz and Bauer, the nasty whispers exchanged on Beach Street, the fierce, hateful glares when their paths crossed. Liz never backed down. She kept The Sand Dollar open, fighting for every sale, every customer. And then there was Bauer, opening his own shop just steps away and selling nearly the same things, stubbornly refusing to change his inventory, as if he were trying to replace her piece by piece.

And then there was the matter of money. Word around town said Liz had owed Bauer a hefty sum of ten thousand dollars from the final messy year they'd spent as business partners. That debt was a sticking point, a festering wound neither of them could ignore. When Ava stepped into the picture, the arguments over money got even worse. People said Ava pushed Bauer to collect, to make Liz pay up or pay the price. There were talks that Ava gave Bauer an ultimatum regarding the situation. Force Liz to pay up and close, or she'd leave him.

And now . . . Liz was gone. Poisoned. Murdered? Maybe suicide? An accident? The whispers of her killing herself felt wrong. Fake. She wasn't fragile, or hopeless, or defeated. She'd seemed frustrated, sure. Angry, definitely. But never broken.

I shook my head, rubbing my temples as if I could massage the swirling thoughts into order. Ava. Bauer. The bitter split. The debt rumors. And now lacing Liz's system, her veins pumping poison throughout her body?

I set the tea down and pulled my knees up to my chest, staring out the dark window at the quiet street below.

*

This Week on the Dunes: A Summer Season Update

A Heavy Heart for Coral Haven

It's with the heaviest of hearts that I write this today. Our town lost one of its own—Elizabeth Carper.

Out of respect for her family and friends, give those closest to her the space and privacy they need as we all try to process the news.

As Detective Hensley confirmed, the investigation is ongoing with no named suspects (however, persons of interest have been identified). The town is watching Bauer and Ava closely, wondering what secrets might still be hiding behind The Shore Thing's bright windows.

The Shore Thing Is Surely Buzzing

With the mysterious death of Elizabeth Carper, the town is buzzing with speculation. Amid the tension, one thing is clear—business is booming at The Shore Thing. Bauer and his girlfriend Ava officially reopened their shop, and foot traffic hasn't slowed. Some customers are drawn by curiosity and are eager to see if the pair give off any "murderous vibes," as one shopper whispered, while others simply want the new summer merchandise. Regardless, sales are up. Many have also commented on how eerily similar some of the store's offerings are to those once featured at The Sand Dollar.

Fireworks Kick Off Early This Year!
The island's about to burst into full-on Fourth of July mode, and trust me, it's going to be loud, sunny, and very, very sparkly.

On **July 3**, head down to the south side of the island for the first round of fireworks. They'll light up right when the sun sets—so bring a blanket, something cold to sip, and a camera. The view over the water is unreal.

Then on **July 4**, get ready for an all-day celebration. Beach Street will be completely closed to traffic and turned into one big summer block party. Expect live bands on every other corner, face painting, a Ferris wheel, and yes—a dunk tank (rumor has it the mayor's volunteering again this year).

For the grown-ups, it's a paradise of orange crushes, light beer, and zero guilt. The smell of grilled shrimp and corn dogs will be the official scent of the day.

And when the sun dips below the horizon, grab a spot on the sand. The main fireworks show will launch from the huge barge just offshore. You'll see the colors ripple across the waves like liquid fire.

And a **brief note for locals and visitors**: A heat advisory has been issued for the upcoming week. Temperatures are expected to climb into the high 90s with strong humidity, so be sure to stay hydrated, limit outdoor activities during peak afternoon hours, and take advantage of the cool breeze near the shoreline.

Stay tuned, Beach Street readers! This story is far from over, and so is the summer heat.

—Claire Bear

FIFTEEN

The walk to the mailbox in the morning was dewy and humid. I grabbed the paper, then meandered back inside and poured some stale coffee into my Shrek mug while letting out the world's longest yawn. I unfolded the latest edition of the *Beach Street Gazette*, the crisp paper dry and thin between my fingers. The front-page headline stared back at me in block letters that seemed to shine beneath the sunlight:

LOCAL SHOP OWNER DEATH STILL UNSOLVED: HOMICIDE OR SUICIDE?

The words alone made my head hurt.

I read the opening lines once, then again, the print swimming as the realization sank in. The article confirmed what the whispers hadn't been able to: Liz Carper was dead by poison. The expedited toxicology report showed traces of bromadiolone, a chemical compound most commonly used in household products like rat poison.

I sipped my coffee. Remembered the women's whispers at The Driftwood. They had been 100 percent *incorrect,* blabbering assholes.

The paper crackled as I tightened my grip, my hands taut. The article continued: Fast-tracked fingerprint analysis and DNA kits were still being processed at the county lab. The crime scene was under full investigation, with the *entire* county police force involved, from the patrol officers who'd sealed off Beach Street that morning to the specialized forensic team extracted from two towns over.

They were still combing through The Sand Dollar piece by piece: black powder dusted on every surface, evidence markers peppering the floor, photographs of glass bottles, ledgers, and faint stains lifted from the counter. Even the back-alley trash bins had been hauled off for testing.

Detective Natalie Hensley, who had since become a familiar face around Coral Haven, was quoted as the lead investigator on Liz's case.

"We're investigating both homicide and suicide at this time," she said. "The scene looked far too neat to be natural. There were no commercial poisonous products present and no clear indication of how the substance was ingested."

The article mentioned that the poison, bromadiolone, was slow-acting—symptoms could take hours to appear, sometimes days. Liz might not even have realized what was happening until it was too late. My spine straightened as I imagined her alone in the shop, working, trusting the air around her while something inside her body quietly shut down.

A photo accompanied by the article: The Sand Dollar, taped off and empty. The camera had caught it midmorning, shadows looming against the pavement, the interior dark and lifeless. The caption read: *Forensic analysis ongoing. No arrests made.*

Even in print, it looked wrong; eerie, hollow, stripped of everything that once made it hers.

Below that, the *Gazette* had used a small inset: Liz's Myspace profile photo smiling on the jetty, hair caught in the wind, sunlight glinting off her eyes. The contrast was brutal. That face, so alive, paired with words like *toxicology* and *poison* and *staged*.

I could almost hear her voice in my head, always calm, deliberate, that faint whistle she did when she was thinking through a display idea. It felt impossible that she was gone, reduced to paragraphs and speculation.

The paper quoted Hensley again:

"We're collecting evidence from every nearby business, reviewing security footage, and taking statements from anyone who interacted with Ms. Carper in her last seventy-two hours alive."

The piece didn't say names, but everyone in town already knew who those people were. Bauer and Ava, the "rival" store owners who'd been questioned at least twice already. Word spread that their shop had been doing well. Some people swore they'd seen Bauer's car parked near the boardwalk late that night. Others said Ava had gone quiet, hiding out until the swell of news calmed.

But then came the question that everyone whispered, even if no one dared to ask it out loud:

Would a rivalry between boutiques really drive someone to murder?

Was Liz killed over competition? Over money? Love? Jealousy? Or something deeper that none of us had seen coming?

I set the paper down, but the headlines still burned behind my eyes.

The rumors had felt like noise. Harmless, even exciting in the way small-town drama could be. But now, there was no escaping the weight of it. This was a body, a crime scene, a chemical compound with a name I'd never heard before and would never forget.

SIXTEEN

In a misguided attempt at self-care, I went to the beach.

The sky was offensively perfect. Clear, blue, smug about it, with a soft breeze and a UV index hovering at a responsible nine. The weather designed for relaxation, bad decisions, and pretending your town wasn't quietly unraveling into a true crime documentary.

Desperate to shake off the grim weight around town, I agreed to meet some of my friends down at the beach. We laid blankets on the sand near our usual spot, passing around cold wine spritzers while gossip swirled in soft bursts. I tried to laugh, tried to care about the usual talk of summer flings and weekend plans, but my mind kept dragging me back to Liz. Her boutique. The poison.

"You know what's weird?" Colleen said, popping a grape into her mouth. "Adam. He's been hanging around

Bauer's shop a lot. Like . . . a lot. They haven't hung out since middle school. So random."

Colleen drifted in and out of the group when her schedule allowed. Due to her forever fluctuating real estate meetings, she wasn't always around, but when she was, she fit in as naturally as if she'd never missed a beat.

"Yeah," Mads added, sipping her wine spritzer. "I saw him there last week, pretending to help, but he was totally just annoying Bauer and Ava the whole time. He thinks he is the shit because Bauer complimented him on his motorcycle one time. ONE time."

"I swear, he wants to be Bauer, like, crawl into his skin," Colleen said. "Or maybe he wants to bang Ava. He practically gets hard when she walks by."

We cackled and hehe'd. Then our playful teasing turned to the rest of town. The way it always did when the sun was warm and the drinks were cold.

"And what about Carol from the Seaside Bakery?" Madison said with a wicked grin. "I swear she's been dying her hair that same shade of bright red since 1998."

Colleen snorted. "Maybe she has a lifetime supply of Redken Red hidden in her basement."

"Or maybe she just wants to look like a drugged-out psychic medium," I chimed in, giggling. "Carol of the Coven Bakery. Watch out, or she'll conjure demons to haunt you. Always lurking, always watching."

We all burst out laughing. It felt good, a rare kind of harmless, ridiculous teasing that only close friends could get away with.

"Oh, and did you see old Mr. Peters jogging on the beach yesterday?" Colleen gasped between laughs. "I think he thinks his eighties workout gear is back in style. The blue matching sweatsuit is bold."

"C'mon, I think he looks sexy," Madison said sarcastically, wiping her eyes.

More laughter rippled over the group, loosening something tight in my chest. Momentarily, the shadow of Liz's death felt far away.

Then Adam rode up on his bike.

He strolled across the sand like he owned it. Nobody seemed surprised to see him.

"Hey Carly, hey guys!" he said with a casual nod, dropping his bag onto the blanket beside us.

"Crazy about Liz's updates, huh? Have you been keeping up with the news?" he said after cracking open a beer. "What a mess. Still, this is probably better for Bauer, right? I mean, her being gone clears the way for his store to really take off. No more competition."

The group quieted. Obviously, the conversation being way too soon after the circumstances. I stared at him, trying to read his face behind those dark shades. He sipped his drink, unbothered.

"What? It's true," he said softly. "He's got the prime location now and no Liz to fight him anymore."

The others shifted uncomfortably. Someone murmured about how it was "too soon" to talk like that, but Adam just shrugged, tossing a broken shell into the sand. Not realizing the severity of his words.

"I'm just saying . . . Bauer's gonna do great. You'll see." Adam said cockily.

"Maybe you want to run Bauer's shop more than he does," Colleen muttered, earning a soft giggle from Madison.

Adam just grinned.

"And Ava," Madison added, teasing. "I bet you wanna smash her, huh?"

Colleen and I both turned to Madison, kind of stunned by her bluntness.

Adam's grin stretched wider, but something dark flickered behind his eyes. "Who wouldn't?" he said lightly. "She's a force. But everyone has their weakness."

He punctuated it with a wink.

SEVENTEEN

The tide rolled forward.

Bauer and Ava were grooving at The Shore Thing, and every head on the street turns when they arrive each morning. People pause mid-conversation, leaning against benches and potted plants or pretending to adjust their sunspecs, just to watch them unlock the door.

From the outside, The Shore Thing looked like it belonged in a glossy travel magazine. It was sharp, with white trim, glass doors, and the faint smell of whiskey and new money every time you walked by. Inside, it was clear Ava knew what she was doing. You could tell she'd worked in retail before. Her efficiency, her sense of layout, even the way she folded a stack of shirts looked methodical, like every corner and shelf had a purpose. The color palette was the opposite of The Sand Dollar: crisp whites, cool grays, touches of navy and gold where Liz preferred sea-glass blues and driftwood tones. Bauer had gone for open space. Clean lines, wide aisles, wrought-iron displays instead of wicker baskets. Even the hangers were branded with the shop's name, *The Shore Thing* etched in sleek script. Three surround sound speakers were tucked into the ceiling, filling the space with soft French pop that made the whole place feel ritzy, like you should be shopping with a mimosa in hand.

I hated to admit it, but the store was stunning. Seamless. Polished. A place that made tourists stop in their tracks and enter.

Still, as I lingered near the window, watching Ava rearrange a mannequin with effortless confidence while Bauer adjusted a display across the room, a small knot twisted in my gut. The shop wasn't so much different from Liz's as it was translated into another dialect. Where Liz leaned organic—driftwood stands, handmade candles, soft linens, a little woo-woo in the best way—Ava stripped everything down to clean lines and empty space.

The merchandise was almost identical: the same elevated basics, the same coastal luxury. But here, an organic cotton blouse hung on a sleek mannequin paired with a simple gold necklace, all restraint and polish. At The Sand Dollar, it would've been folded beside a Himalayan salt lamp and a bundle of dried eucalyptus.

I admired the vision, the taste, the precision of it all.

From my perch at The Driftwood's front window, I kept staring. Bauer's face was drawn and tense, his usual grin replaced by thin lips and fast glances over his shoulder. Ava, always so put-together, kept flicking her hair and scanning the sidewalk as if on the defense, daring anyone to approach. The usual confidence she carried seemed forced today, brittle at the edges.

Detective Hensley showed up not long after they opened, stepping right into the shop with a quiet authority that made heads turn. One by one, Bauer and Ava were pulled aside to speak to her, again. The tension was thick as sea mist. It was clear the police weren't letting them off their radar just yet. I was almost positive that Hensley was going to escort them to the station, but their interaction was civil, calm. Uninteresting.

*

Bauer and Ava's business boomed. A steady stream of customers wandered into The Shore Thing, bags swinging as they exited, faces animated with excitement. New sun hats, braided necklaces, and the occasional volleyball set were all nearly identical to what Liz once sold at The Sand Dollar. Whispers drifted out with every shopper:

"Isn't this like the same stuff the store down the street used to have?"

"It feels weird . . . but the prices are good, and it smells amazing inside."

"I heard they're trying to replace The Sand Dollar inventory completely."

Even with all the tension surrounding Bauer and Ava, their shop was thriving. Maybe even more so because of the murder. People wanted to see the drama, buy the goods, and feel like they were part of the scandal.

EIGHTEEN

People don't come together like this unless something has gone terribly wrong.

The community gathered on the steps of Coral Haven Town Hall, drawn by the promise of answers. It was rare to see this many people in one place outside of the Fourth of July parade or the annual Strawberry Festival but today wasn't about celebration. Today was about loss. It was solely about Liz.

The crowd pressed closer, the air thick with humidity and nerves. News trucks lined the curb; satellite dishes angled toward the sky. Camera crews adjusted tripods and lights, wires snaking across the sidewalk like roots. Reporters murmured rehearsed intros to their microphones, waiting for the sound bite that would make the evening broadcast.

I wedged myself between Mrs. Tropez from the local animal shelter and two teenage boys from the surf rental place. The whispers of speculation quieted as Detective Hensley stepped up to the hastily assembled podium. Her uniform was immaculate despite the heat, her hair pulled back in that severe bun I'd come to associate with her.

When she spoke, her voice carried easily through the static of the news mics.

"Good afternoon. As of this morning, the investigation into the death of Elizabeth Carper remains active and ongoing. At this stage, we are treating the case as a probable homicide."

A ripple ran through the crowd. Quick breaths, muted exclamations.

Hensley paused just long enough for the silence to settle before continuing. "The scene at The Sand Dollar does not align with a clear-cut suicide. Toxicology reports have confirmed the presence of bromadiolone, a highly toxic anticoagulant commonly known as rat poison, in Ms. Carper's system. The lack of a farewell note and lack of circumstantial evidence for a suicide makes the case point to homicide. There were no external injuries and no signs of forced entry or struggle. Because of this, we suspect Liz may have known the possible assailant."

The press erupted. Shutters clicked. Reporters called out questions over one another, their words tangling in the open coastal air.

"Detective, do you have a suspect?"
"Was this deliberate or accidental exposure?"
"Are local businesses under investigation?"

Hensley lifted a hand for calm. "We continue to pursue all leads currently. We ask the public to refrain from speculation and to contact authorities with any relevant information."

Her gaze swept over the crowd. Stern, steady, unflinching.

"Ms. Carper was a valued member of this community. Our department is committed to finding answers for her family and for the people of Coral Haven."

Immediately, reporters were barking questions, locals whispering theories, an aura of grief and curiosity colliding in the humid air.

I didn't move. My heart thudded in my chest. Liz's cause of death wasn't just gossip anymore. It was official. It was murder.

The crowd loitered, restless and buzzing. Behind me, someone whispered, "It had to be someone she knew. Someone who she befriended or trusted."

I swallowed hard, glancing toward Beach Street, toward The Shore Thing, wondering if the killer had walked right past me that morning.

NINETEEN

I couldn't free myself from the relentless anxiety after the press conference, the questions, the whispers, the unfinished words. I found myself walking down Beach Street and I wandered curiously toward The Shore Thing, trying to understand the allure.

I stepped inside, letting the bells above the door chime softly. Bauer was at the counter, bagging up a few items for a customer, covering each item in black tissue paper, his eyes shadowed with exhaustion. He didn't acknowledge me. Ava stood near the fitting room hallway, phone pressed to her ear, pacing. I drifted closer to a rack of sundresses, trying to browse but also straining to catch her voice.

"No, I told you . . . I had nothing to do with it," Ava hissed into the phone, her voice sharp and low. "I hated her, sure. But not enough to kill her. You think I'd be that stupid? With this whole town watching? Yes, yes."

There was a pause. Her heels clicked softly on the hardwood floor.

"Because they're all looking at us now. The police, the detective, the customers—everyone. And Bauer's a wreck. It wasn't supposed to happen like this."

Another pause.

"No, I don't care what Liz said. She pushed us way too far; she deserved to be hit with some bad luck, but not like this. Not dead."

Ava glanced over her shoulder, forcing a bright smile at a group of shoppers wandering in, before turning away and lowering her voice again.

"I told you, that is sensitive information that we shouldn't discuss over the telephone. Don't call me here again."

She hung up, slipping her phone into her shoulder bag and adjusting a stack of folded tank tops on the display table like nothing had happened.

I turned, staring at a rack of gold earrings, my heart thudding hard in my chest. Her words rang in my ears. She hated Liz. She admitted it. But was that enough to kill her?

Bauer's laugh, forced and hollow, floated from the register as he handed a bag to a customer. Thanking them for their support. The shop buzzed with life, but behind the pretty displays and bright smiles, the tension was suffocating.

I left quickly, the bells chiming behind me, excited to do some more snooping.

*

My suspicion of Ava only grew after overhearing that phone call, it being clipped, strained. Who really knew her? What did any of us actually know about the woman who'd appeared so suddenly in Coral Haven and managed to stitch herself seamlessly into Bauer's life and business?

The chance to get a fresh scoop for the blog sent me to the local library. I needed Wi-Fi. I was already downtown, and it was closer than biking home to grab my laptop.

The library sat just off Main Street, tucked behind the community center. Its weathered sign creaked in the breeze, the painted letters slightly faded from years of salt air. Inside, it smelled faintly of old paper, with a distinct blend of locals and tourists who wandered in to escape the heat.

The space was cozy but a little cluttered. Pale-yellow walls framed rows of tall, squeaky shelves packed with everything from battered beach reads to encyclopedias that hadn't been opened in a decade. A few kids were sprawled in the children's section, sunburnt noses peeling as they chortled through picture books, their laughter bouncing softly off the walls. Their parents hovered nearby, pretending to browse the endless spines of Coral Haven's modest book collection, but really just waiting for story time to end.

I chose a computer station near the back, one of six aging desktops whirring faintly beneath a fluorescent light. The monitor took a full minute to boot up, long enough for me to notice a man two seats down scrolling through a recipe for slow pork roast, his screen glowing warmly in the dimness.

When my browser finally loaded, I cracked my knuckles and typed in a few searches.

Ava Delaney.
Ava Delaney previous employment.
Ava Delaney criminal charges.

Something odd surfaced.

An archived news article, buried under layers of results, mentioned Ava working for a high-end department store out of state. She'd been on track for a major promotion—impressive title, glowing reviews—until tragedy hit. One of her coworkers had died unexpectedly. The details were scarce, but there were whispers of workplace tension, disagreements, rumors that never quite reached print.

After that, Ava disappeared from the company records. No farewell announcement, no transfer. Just . . . gone.

I leaned closer to the screen, squinting my eyes. The parallels were impossible to ignore. A sudden departure, a new beginning in a small town, a new relationship, and now another death wrapped in mystery.

The library's air conditioning clicked on overhead, rattling slightly in the ceiling vents. The sound made me jump. Around me, a little girl laughed loudly at a storybook character, her mom shushing her with a gentle hand. Life went on, perfectly normal.

I pressed the print button and started to collect the information. I sat back in the plastic office chair, the cursor blinking on the search bar, my reflection faint in the glass of the monitor.

TWENTY

I waited outside the town's police station, adjusting my backpack slung on my shoulder while scanning and searching for Detective Hensley's arrival. When I saw her unmarked police cruiser pull up along Beach Street, my heart thumped nervously. This was probably a terrible idea and intrusive to the investigation, but I couldn't shake what I'd found out about Ava. Someone needed to know.

As Detective Hensley stepped onto the sidewalk, I hurried toward her. "Detective, can I have a minute?" I asked, trying to sound casual.

She sighed and glanced at her watch. "Claire, unless you have something new for the investigation—real evidence—I can't waste time on gossip."

"This isn't gossip, I swear," I insisted, lowering my voice. "I found something about Ava's past. Before she moved here, she worked at a big department store, right?

After scanning through some articles, I found out that she was up for a promotion when one of her coworkers mysteriously died. And right after that, she left the company. It's all in old news clippings." I pointed at the manila folder I was holding.

For a long moment, Detective Hensley said nothing, then she grabbed the folder full of my neatly printed research. Her gaze narrowed, studying me with fresh interest, but then her professional mask slid back into place.

"Claire, no offense, but stay in your lane. Let us handle this. You're not qualified. You're not a detective, let alone an officer," she said curtly. "Don't get yourself tangled up in something dangerous."

I swallowed the lump in my throat and nodded, forcing myself to walk away down the street. But as I glanced back over my shoulder, I caught Hensley pulling out her phone, her expression thoughtful.

*

After my unsuccessful visit to the police station, I went straight home to de-stress and write. I sat cross-legged on my living room floor, surrounded by a sea of papers. Colorful sketches, rough drafts, character ideas. All meant for the children's book I'd dreamed of writing since moving to Coral Haven. My coffee table was buried under the clutter, a half-finished mug of tea teetering dangerously close to the edge.

But no matter how hard I tried to focus, my mind kept drifting back to Liz. To Bauer. To Ava. To the eerie threads weaving themselves into the fabric of this town's darkest story. My pencil hovered over a page, the outline of a curious little jellyfish left unfinished.

With a frustrated sigh, I dropped the pencil and leaned back, letting my head rest against the couch. "Get it together, Claire," I muttered.

I made a mental note to check in with Carly, Madison, and Olivia to see how they were handling all this madness. Maybe they'd heard something new around town, a rumor or slip of gossip I could quietly tuck into my mental files.

But for now, the cozy, safe, magical world of children's storytelling would have to wait. A real-life catastrophe had taken over.

*

This Week on the Dunes: Humidity, Happenings & Happy Hour

Hey Coral Haven crew! Hope you're all staying cool out there. The humidity has officially declared itself our fourth season, and my hair has fully surrendered to it.

This week, there's actually so much happening around town that I had to break out my trusty planner (yes, the paper kind) just to keep track. Here's what's coming up on the dunes:

Butterflies, Binoculars & Benefiting the Parks!

Our beloved Science Center is hosting a pop-up butterfly exhibit starting Friday morning. Expect tropical species, fun photo ops, and air conditioning (arguably the best part). While you're there, don't miss Saturday's **Bird Watching for a Cause** event—all donations go directly to the Parks & Rec Department to keep our beaches, trails, and dunes pristine. Bring your binoculars, your iced coffee, and your patience; the ospreys like to play hard to get.

Sidewalk Sale Season

Mark your calendars for this upcoming weekend! Several Beach Street boutiques are rolling out major discounts. Rumor has it that even the fancier shops are participating this year, so it's the perfect time to snag that sundress or pair of sandals you've been eyeing since Memorial Day. Just don't forget sunscreen—retail therapy is best enjoyed without tan lines.

Restaurant Week Is Back!
It's finally here! Grab a friend, a date, or an excuse and check out the menus posted in front of your favorite restaurants. The chefs have outdone themselves this season, offering three-course specials that'll make you forget you ever owned a microwave. A quick tip: Make reservations early. They fill up faster than a cooler at sunrise.

And as for Liz's Case...
The latest from the investigation confirms what many of us feared: Liz Carper's sudden death was no accident. Toxicology reports revealed traces of rat poison in her system—the kind no one accidentally stirs into their morning latte. Police are treating this as a likely homicide. Coral Haven may be small, but secrets here can be deadly.

Until next time, take a walk, tip your servers, and try to find the good in the small things.

See you on the dunes,
—Claire Bear

TWENTY-ONE

Restaurant Week had officially begun, which meant all rules were temporarily suspended.

After a full day of work and far too much mindless TV, I was more than ready to be lured back into civilization. Olivia texted me: *I'm starving. Restaurant Week is calling. Let's all pretend we're fancy.* That was all the convincing I needed. Twenty minutes later, we were riding our beach cruiser bikes with no cares in the world.

We ended up at Fin Inn, one of the pricier spots just off Beach Street that was offering the coveted three-course special, only sixty dollars, wine not included, but worth every penny. The host squeezed us in last minute, a miracle for Restaurant Week.

The tablecloth was crisp white, the lighting dim enough to make everyone squint to read the menu. We ordered a basket of warm bread for the table, glossy with olive oil, and a bottle of something dry and sparkling that none of us could pronounce.

I went with a Caesar salad to start, cold with lemon—followed by sea bass so tender it flaked at the touch of a fork. Dessert was a perfect little chocolate mousse that came with an espresso on the side, rich enough to wake the dead.

Madison sighed dramatically after a sip of wine. "Okay, this is my official vacation from all things depressing."

"Seconded," Olivia said, tearing another piece of bread. "No Liz talk. No Bauer talk. None of that shit, especially no suspects. Only carbs and alcohol."

Colleen nodded. "And if anyone says the word *toxicology*, I'm throwing them into the ocean with cinder blocks tied to their legs."

We laughed, like really laughed. The sound almost felt strange, rusty around the edges.

Still, even with the good food and the soft music, there was the invisible tightness. The restaurant was full of low buzzes of speculation and gossip that seemed to follow us everywhere lately. Every so often I'd catch a word, "police," "investigation," "Bauer," and I'd force myself to look away.

Then, mercifully, something else caught our attention.

At the table beside us, a couple was unraveling in spectacular fashion. The woman, all red lipstick and gaudy bracelets, jabbed a manicured finger across the table. "You know what your problem is? You're a total suck-up, momma's boy. You do everything she tells you and nothing I ask, you piece of shit."

The man leaned forward, voice low but sharp. "You're making a scene. Can you not?"

"Don't you dare shush me, Evan."

Colleen froze, mid-bite. "Oh my God," she whispered with a slightly maniacal grin. "Is this happening right now?"

It was. It absolutely was. The man muttered something, something that definitely included the word "bitch," and before any of us could blink, she snatched up her water glass and threw it straight in his face.

The splash was glorious.

Madison clapped a hand over her mouth to keep from laughing. Olivia, wide-eyed, reached for the wine bottle. "We're gonna need a refill for this. Open the other bottle."

We all leaned in, watching the chaos unfold. The soaked man sputtered something about "embarrassment" and "cab," while the woman stormed past us toward the door, her heels clicking like punctuation marks.

We sat in stunned silence, and then Colleen raised her glass. "To those strangers and their amazing public meltdown," she said.

We all drank—a lot—to that. We were grateful, in a strange way, to be spectators of drama where no one got hurt.

*

It was a random, late afternoon when a knock came at my bungalow apartment door. I was in the middle of potting some herbs; I wiped my soil-covered hands on a soapy dish towel and peeked through the oval window. My heart gave an uneasy jump. Detective Hensley stood outside, looking surprisingly casual, her hands tucked into the pockets of her jacket. Her undercover police cruiser was parked in front of the property.

Hesitantly, I opened the door. "Detective?" I said with confusion, my voice an octave higher.

"Claire," she said with a nod. "Mind if I come in for a minute?"

"Uh, of course."

She stepped inside, glancing briefly around my small but cozy coastal living room.

"I wanted to apologize," she began. "You were right about Ava. I must confirm or deny every possible lead, so I did some of my own research—thank you for the head start—and I found the articles you mentioned about her job, the promotion she was fighting for, and her coworker's unexplained death. It's . . . concerning. More than I thought. Similar, similar enough to fully investigate."

Detective Hensley explained more: suspicious death of a coworker, potential rivalry for a promotion. No charges had been filed. No foul play, officially.

I crossed my arms, the nerves settling into curiosity. "You believe me now? Also, how rude of me . . . Do you want coffee, tea, fruit punch?"

Hensley gave a thin smile, caught off guard. "Hm, no . . . thank you." She paused. "I believe you have good instincts. And you're more tuned in to this town than most—especially with that Myspace blog of yours. Yes,

I've been studying your entries. Which brings me to why I'm here."

I raised an eyebrow. "My blog?"

"I was wrong to dismiss you so abruptly. You've got your ear to the ground. The locals talk to you, they trust you. They spill things they wouldn't tell the police," she said. "If you hear anything—anything that sounds off, especially connected to Liz's case—I want you to come to me first."

"You want me to work for you for free?" I teased, half-joking.

She gave a small laugh and quickly became stern. "I want you to keep your ears open. And keep me in the loop. No publishing any rumors that could damage the investigation, understand?"

I nodded slowly, feeling a strange mix of pride and unease. "Deal."

"Good." Hensley turned to leave, then paused at the door. "Oh—and keep your head down, Claire. Whoever did this . . . they're still out there."

*

This Week on the Dunes: Town Terrors?

So, if you were anywhere near the boardwalk last night, you probably saw the flashing lights, the crowd, and heard the screams that were thankfully not from terror, but from . . . boredom?

The Boardwalk Roller Coaster Incident (Everyone's Okay!)
Yep—our beloved Tidal Rush roller coaster decided it needed a little mid-ride nap. The cars stalled right at the top of the loop (of course it did) with twenty brave riders dangling in the air for almost thirty minutes. Can you imagine? Half an hour just . . . hanging out, thirty feet above the boardwalk, waving at seagulls and trying not to think about gravity.

Luckily, the weather was gorgeous, and everyone stayed calm. The maintenance crew handled it with no injuries, no trauma, just some shaky knees and dramatic selfies once everyone was back on solid ground. The best part? The Tidal Rush is already back up and running after a quick fix and inspection this morning. Talk about resilience.

Paws & Play Coming Next Summer!

Now for the cutest news of the week. The town council officially approved permits for Coral Haven's first-ever dog park! It'll open next summer inland near Seabreeze Avenue. Expect sod grass (no more muddy paws!), a sparkling new water fountain, a mini agility course with tunnels and ramps, and shaded benches for all the puppy parents to rest. This has been a long time coming—I can already see the Facebook posts!

Ink & Inspiration—Tattoo Convention This Weekend!

For my fellow art lovers (and spontaneous souls), the Coastal Ink Expo is rolling into the Convention Center this Saturday and Sunday! Come see some of the best tattoo artists from all over the East Coast, grab a flash tattoo, or just check out the live demos. There'll be prizes, raffles, and free piercings for early attendees. If you see me wandering around the vendor booths—no, I'm not getting a shark tattoo. Probably.

It's shaping up to be another wild week in Coral Haven: a little adrenaline, a little art, and a whole lot of community.

Stay curious, stay caffeinated, and please, double-check your seat belts.

—Claire Bear

TWENTY-TWO

At some point, curiosity stops being innocent.

I took a slow walk down the back roads to get to my shift, past the cluster of shops that framed The Sand Dollar. The police tape was long gone now. I stopped in a few stores under the guise of shopping. Picking up a painting here, pretending to browse postcards there, all while quietly testing the waters.

"Did you see anything that morning?" I asked a few of the owners, keeping my tone light, conversational. "Anyone hanging around who didn't belong?"

Most of them gave polite, clipped answers. A few just shrugged, their eyes darting toward the door like they couldn't wait for me to leave. Nobody wanted to talk.

I stopped into the cooking store next to the old surf shop. The owner, Mrs. Travers, wiped her hands on her apron and frowned at me. "You're not the police, Claire," she said quietly, her voice firm but not unkind. "You should stop asking questions before someone thinks you know more than you do."

But I didn't want to stop.

*

I was working my shift when the familiar voices of Carly and Olivia echoed through the doorway. They came in, grinning and still sweaty from Carly's morning Pilates class, embracing me in their gross, wet hugs. They both were wearing expensive workout clothes and kept blotting themselves with already soaked towels. Olivia put down their gear and slid comfortably into one of the booths in my section.

"Hello darling, help me. Carly completely killed us this morning in class. Ice-cold water, please, chop-chop now," Olivia said, fanning herself dramatically. "And maybe a smoothie that's 'off the menu' if you've got protein powder and extra berries. Tell Sean in the kitchen that I said hi." Olivia had the biggest crush on The Driftwood's scummy sous chef.

"Coming right up, and ew, no. Seriously?" I said, uncontrollably grinning at my friends and grabbing my notepad. Carly leaned across the table, her eyes gleaming.

She was practically foaming at the mouth when she started speaking. "Claire, you won't believe what we saw last night," she said in a voice of disbelief. "We went to the dive bar for fifty-cent wings, and guess who was there? Bauer. And Adam."

I paused, drinks only half filled. "Together, just the two of them? I didn't know they were close like that."

"Yep, they were super close during middle school," Olivia confirmed. "Anyway, Bauer was totally messed up, swaying on his stool, grieving Liz, seeming conflicted. How he couldn't believe she was really gone. How messed up it all is because she was his ex-fiancée. You could tell he was spiraling. It was quite sad. Taking vodka shots by himself."

"Sad. And Adam . . ." Carly trailed off. "He was just sitting there. Consoling Bauer and listening to every word. Like he was soaking it all in, almost ecstatic that Bauer was confiding in him. Honestly, it was a little over-the-top and dramatic . . ."

Before I could press for more, the entry door swung open and in walked Adam, sporting worn-in blue jeans and a black T-shirt with the name of his family's business, Morgan Family Winery.

Adam scanned the crowd, looking for a familiar face. Seeing us, he smiled and made a beeline for Carly and Olivia's booth. "Mind if I join you, ladies?"

Of course they didn't mind, he was a harmless guy who just wanted friends, but his arrival did interrupt our hangout.

The table fell awkwardly silent. Carly stiffened, glancing at me with wide eyes; Olivia quickly greeted Adam and began small talk before the silence lasted too long. I felt my Razr buzz and noticed a new message from Carly.

I glanced down and read: *I'll tell u the rest l8r*

*

My shift at The Driftwood was finally over, I glanced at the time and sighed. I'd promised to babysit that evening for the Strano family, a family that spends each summer here. Their five-year-old son, Caden, was full of energy and had already worn me out the last time I sat for him. I texted Carly as I gathered my things: *Babysitting til 10. Call u around 9.*

The Stranos' rental house was cozy and packed with sandy beach gear. Caden greeted me with his usual whirlwind excitement, dragging out a tower of Jenga blocks, his Yu-Gi-Oh cards, and the family's old Nintendo system before I could even get my shoes off.

"Can we watch *Toy Story* again? And then play *Mario Kart*?"

"Sure, Cay," I said while messing up his hair, and I settled in for the long haul.

Two Disney movies, a round of Jenga, and a couple heated *Mario Kart* tournaments later, Caden was finally tucked into bed, snuggled under pirate-themed sheets. I tiptoed out of his room, quietly descended the stairs, and pulled out my phone to call Carly.

"Hey!" she practically shouted, picking up immediately. "I'm so glad you called. I wanted to finish telling you about last night."

"I'm all ears," I said, curling up on the Stranos' couch and munching on leftover popcorn that lay in a bowl on the wooden coffee table.

"Where did we stop . . . Okay, yes, Adam and Bauer were sitting at the bar. Bauer was super drunk. He was slurring, rambling, totally out of it. And Adam? He was soaking it all up like it was a freaking Sunday sermon."

"What was Bauer actually saying, like what were his words?" I asked, holding my breath.

"He was going on about Liz. How angry he was that she never paid him back the ten grand she owed him. He said she was being ungodly stubborn. Then—and this is the weird part—he started muttering about Ava. About how much Ava hated Liz. Like . . . really hated her. But I think he realized he needed to shut up. He ordered another shot and rapidly became too drunk to even speak."

I sat up straighter. "Woah, wait. Hated her enough to kill her?"

"Well," Carly said, her voice dropping to a whisper, "that's the thing. Bauer was saying he was mad at Liz, but that he'd never do anything violent to her. But Ava? He sounded like he feared what Ava might've been capable of. Like he wouldn't put it past her if she'd done something crazy."

"That's . . . interesting. Do you think he's trying to shift blame?" I breathed. Swiping my hand down my face, getting a tad bit exhausted with the influx of info I was hearing.

"I'm not sure. Then Adam said something else I think?" Carly added. "He told Bauer that love and money are the two biggest motives for murder. Like he was just casually dropping that into the conversation. But that's not all," Carly continued. "Right after that, Adam leaned in and asked Bauer if Liz had any enemies, current boyfriends, or people holding grudges that they should be worried about."

I frowned. "Seriously? Do you think Bauer feels guilty?" I wondered aloud. "Maybe he thinks Ava lost control. Or maybe his own actions are finally catching up to him?"

"Exactly. It was like he was trying to convince himself she couldn't have done it, but deep down . . . he knew she could have. I mean, how much does he really know her? They've been together for what, a whole four months?!"

I rubbed my forehead, a migraine brewing, the length of the day catching up to me.

"Wrong. Six months? Oh, guess what, I have news," I added. "Detective Hensley stopped by my apartment the other day. She apologized for brushing me off about Ava, surprisingly. Said she checked out what I found. And she asked me to keep my ears open for any new gossip— for the investigation."

"No way!" Carly gasped. "Claire, that's huge news. Your blog is actually helping solve a murder."

"It is not like my blog will crack the case, but it's kind of crazy, right? I still don't believe it," I said, smiling, and laughed softly. "But this is also kind of terrifying."

"Yes, terrifying. Be careful, okay?" Carly warned. "You're getting way too close to all of this."

"I know. But I can't stop now. Not when there's so much left I can find out."

We eventually drifted into lighter topics. Upcoming movies, beach plans, even what color Carly was painting her toenails next. We later hung up and the day caught up to me. All I wanted was to get home, crawl into my own bed, and let the swirling pieces of the day settle.

TWENTY-THREE

Bauer's face lingered for a moment after I woke, warped by the logic of nightmares, before the details slipped away—leaving only that familiar, crawling unease. I stared at the ceiling, heart racing, the night already ruined by a spiral of nonstop thoughts. By morning, I needed a distraction. Something bright.

I texted Madison to see if she wanted to meet at the smoothie cart by the beach lot. She replied within seconds: *Yes plz. I need sun + gossip. Off in 10 min*

By the time she arrived, I was already lounging on the cement ledge near the rusted bike rack, sipping a strawberry fruit smoothie and watching beachgoers rinse the wet sand off their feet, chairs, and toys as their kids threw the most annoying tantrums.

Madison ran up in her scrubs, a bun on top of her head with hairs wisping in the wind and her hospital ID badge swinging with every step, carrying her bikini in one hand and a blanket in the other. "I swear, if one more dumb person walks into the ER with sun poisoning and says, 'But I put some sunscreen on,' I'm going to snap. Why have there been so many skateboarding injuries? Where are they skateboarding?! Does no one know how to hydrate? Oh, hello, my dear."

"Rough shift?" I asked, offering her the extra strawberry smoothie I ordered.

"Rough week," she muttered, flopping beside me. "I've seen enough burns, blisters, sprained ankles, and objects stuffed up butts to last a lifetime. But you're not here for that. I know you want dirt."

I smiled. "Only if you've got it."

"Ugh, you use me," Madison said dramatically. "One sec, Claire. Gotta change."

She ran to the closest comfort station to get beach-ready.

Madison came jogging back, towel tucked under one arm, drink in the other. We meandered to our spot, and she dropped beside me, took a long sip, and leaned in.

"Okay," she said under her breath. "You know how the autopsy came back positive for bromadiolone, right?"

"Right."

"Well . . ." Her voice lowered to almost nothing. "I shouldn't even be saying this, but the toxin didn't just make her sick. It tore her apart from the inside out. Her gums, nose, and . . . anus were bleeding. Her organs were failing, Claire. That shit destroys the body's ability to clot. Once it starts, there's no stopping it."

I froze, the salt wind catching in my throat. "What. The. Fuck. You're serious?"

Madison nodded, eyes fixed on the horizon. "They found signs that it had been building for days. The internal damage was everywhere. It's one of those poisons that makes you look like you've just come down with the flu until it's too late. By the time anyone would've realized . . ." She trailed off.

My stomach turned over. The idea of Liz—bright, sunburned, laughing Liz—slowly unraveling like that made my chest ache. Deteriorating from the inside out.

"And there was alcohol in her system too," Madison added quietly. "A lot. Enough to mask what was happening, maybe even speed it up."

A gull cried overhead, sharp and distant. I wrapped my arms around my knees, staring out at the water.

"So whoever did this," I whispered, "knew exactly what they were doing."

"Right," Madison confirmed. "Get this, rumor is one of the ER docs saw her the week before she died. She came in complaining about stomach pain and nausea. They gave her fluids, ran some tests, but nothing major showed up at the time."

My ears perked up. "Wait, seriously?"

"Yep. But here's where it gets weird. My coworker said that someone called the hospital the next day asking for a copy of her charts. Said they were her *attorney*."

I blinked in confusion. "That's strange. Do you know who called? Who knew she was in the hospital?"

"No name left. I don't even think her parents knew. Unknown number, blocked. Just a voicemail on the admin line. But the voice was male, authoritative, and apparently sounded kind of young. Didn't leave a callback number either."

I stared out at the water, raising my head toward the sun to recharge, my thoughts racing. "Someone knew she wasn't well. And tried to see what was in her medical record?"

"That's what I think."

I looked at Madison. "Could the hospital release that info to just anyone?"

She shook her head. "Nope. HIPAA. In fact, I shouldn't be telling you any of this, so shut your face. Anyway, it would've had to be Liz herself, or someone legally allowed, like her parents. But the request was denied, and they flagged it as suspicious in the system."

I exhaled slowly. "And no one followed up on it?"

"Not that I know of. And officially, we're not supposed to talk about it. But one of the night nurses overheard a few doctors saying it was 'bad timing' and 'awfully coincidental.' The kind of thing they don't write down but mentally make note of."

I nodded, trying to make sense of this newfound information. "Thanks for telling me. Seriously."

Madison gave me a gentle elbow nudge. "Be careful, Claire. We're worried about you. You're deeper into this than you think. And don't say shit."

"I know, I won't," I whispered. "And I don't think I can stop, and I don't think I want to."

She sighed, half amused, half exasperated. "You know we used to talk about normal things, right? Like anything other than what happened to Liz? Now it's just murder, murder, murder with you."

I cracked a small smile. "Sorry. Occupational hazard of being nosy."

Madison shook her head.

We leaned back, letting the sun warm our faces and the ocean breeze smooth out the tension building under our skin. The shoreline was loud with life, waves rolling in, kids shrieking near the jetty, someone laughing way too hard over a portable speaker.

A little farther down the beach, a group of young girls wandered the water's edge, tiny silhouettes against the tides. They bent low, scanning the sand with determined little frowns, choosing only the shells the waves hadn't managed to fracture. Every time one of them found a perfect one, she held it up like a trophy, and the rest crowded around with the kind of joy adults forget how to have.

I watched them for a long moment, wishing I still believed magical things washed ashore that easily.

Beside me, Madison let out a long breath and closed her eyes. I did the same, letting the sun settle on my skin and the steady pull of the tide quiet the noise in my head.

TWENTY-FOUR

I should have been winding down in the comfort of my own home. The lamp in the corner lit the room, its soft amber light flickering against the pale walls like a heartbeat. The dishes were done. My little, almost dead, succulent garden on the sill glistened from a fresh misting. Outside, the neighbor's old dog was snoring gently on the porch across the way. It should've been a peaceful night.

I padded across the rug in my panda slippers, climbed into bed, and tugged my comforter up to my chest. My duvet was white, fluffy, and cool to the touch. It was like wrapping myself in a hotel cloud. Six pillows surrounded me in a fortress of softness, each one fluffed and positioned just the way I liked. My sound machine clicked on, and a low thunderstorm began to rumble faintly through the speakers. Rain without the wetness, thunder without the danger. My version of calm.

The nightstand beside me held a small constellation of my life in photos. Me and the girls at the beach, all drunk smiles and messy hair. My parents standing outside their yellow house holding sparklers, taken at an old birthday party. And one frame tucked in the back, of my college friends, now scattered across the country with kids, mortgages, and real jobs. They'd moved forward; I'd taken an unexpected and different turn, chasing stories and salt air instead of stability. Sometimes that felt like freedom. Sometimes, I reflected on my life in the city and how close I was to having that.

I flipped open my laptop, the screen's blue light washing over the covers, and typed the words I couldn't stop thinking about.

Rat poison homicide.

Dozens of search results blinked to life. I clicked through each one, skimming clinical descriptions, medical reports, true crime snippets.

Deliberate poisoning is a known method of homicide.

Exposure can occur through contaminated water or infected soil. However, in criminal cases, the poison is more commonly ingested through tainted food and drink.

That part hit hardest.

Food. Drink. Hospitality. Things we offered freely in Coral Haven without a second thought—coffee dates, wine nights, welcome treats for tourists. Even awkward reconciliations between exes outside of shops on Beach Street.

The next line in the article made my stomach turn.

A person who has swallowed the product may show signs within thirty minutes. These symptoms include severe stomach pain, diarrhea, drowsiness, headaches, and confusion.

Madison had said Liz had come to the ER with stomach pain and nausea. Nothing major showed up in her tests. They sent her home. Those could've been her first signs, the warning flares everyone missed. How was that possible?

I scrolled farther.

In cases of gradual exposure, the victim may appear increasingly fatigued. Internal bleeding, bruising, and neurological confusion may occur before death.

A chill rippled up my arms.

Just before Liz had died, I'd stopped by The Sand Dollar to replace the last candle I'd burned down to wax and wick. Liz was behind the counter, same as always, but something about her felt . . . off. Her coloring looked pale beneath the shop lights, the usual warmth drained from her face.

"You okay?" I'd asked, setting the candle down.

She waved it off with a thin smile. "Yeah. Just this annoying stomachache. Probably stress. Or karma."

I laughed, because that's what you do when someone says they're fine, right? She rang me up, her fingers trembling just slightly and a bit clammy as she handed me the receipt. I remember thinking she looked tired. Nothing more.

Now, staring at the screen, that memory rewrote itself.

I shut my laptop for a second, pressing my palms against my eyes.

Someone had done this to her. Slowly. Deliberately. Watching her fade from the inside out.

I remembered what Madison had mentioned, a strange call to the hospital. An anonymous caller asking for Liz's chart. A man's voice. Curious, maybe panicked. Whoever it was had left a trace.

I reached for my notebook, the one I usually reserved for story ideas about mermaids and talking seashells. Its pages were lined with doodles of jellyfish, beach crabs, and coral reefs. But this time, I flipped to a blank page.

With my pen poised above the paper, I began writing everything I could remember:
Liz's symptoms.
The possible timeline.
The phone call.
The hospital visit.
Every loose end that suddenly didn't seem so loose anymore.

The thunder coming from my sound machine rolled softly, but I couldn't turn my mind off.

TWENTY-FIVE

Sometimes, the only cure for a crowded mind is an empty horizon.

The sun was slipping low, painting the ocean in streaks of rose gold and silver. I kicked off my sneakers at the edge of the shoreline and let my toes sink into the warm sand. A salty breeze lifted my hair as I walked closer to the waterline, the thin edge of each wave curling over my feet, cool and fleeting, before dissolving back into the sea.

The beach was alive with weekend energy; the "world's best sunsets" brought huge crowds. A group of teenagers had claimed a prime spot near the boardwalk, their compact speaker blasting a throwback pop song that made a few nearby parents shake their heads and sigh. Couples reclined in their beach chairs, perusing paperback beach reads or chatting lazily over chips and beers. Kids shrieked as they ran away from the too-close tide only to end up soaking wet.

I slowed my pace, letting the rhythm of the waves sync with my breath.

But even here, the whispers followed.

"—Bauer's shop is swamped now, everyone's curious," a woman said to her friend, adjusting her oversized beach hat.

"Yeah, and his girlfriend . . . did you see her face on Beach Street? Like she doesn't give a shit that Liz is gone," the friend replied.

My ears caught the drift of every passing comment. Liz's name was a current running under all of it. Bauer. Ava. The Sand Dollar. The Shore Thing. No matter how bright the sun, her absence cast a shadow.

I brushed the wet sand off my ankles and kept walking. Maybe I came to the beach for peace, but I couldn't escape the feeling that this town had been split into two worlds: the Coral Haven that existed before Liz's death, and the one that was obviously unraveling now.

And whether I liked it or not, I was knee-deep in the second one.

*

The next day, I spotted Carly's familiar yellow, straw bucket hat and Olivia's floral towel near the lifeguard stand. They had set up a little oasis with two beach chairs, a cooler tucked into the sand, and a giant striped umbrella flapping lightly in the breeze—although no one was using the shade given by the umbrella. Carly was half-buried in her latest coastal romance paperback, while Olivia had her cell out, squinting, trying to decipher the messages on her phone with the sun glare.

"Look who finally showed up," Carly teased, lowering her sunglasses. "We thought you got swallowed by The Driftwood."

"Not today," I said, flinging my neon-purple jelly slides aside and collapsing onto their blanket. "Needed the ocean and a tan more than I needed tips."

Olivia sat up, brushing sand from her elbows. "Okay, so people aren't getting any less obnoxious. You missed a crowd earlier. Bauer was out walking by the pier. People were literally pointing. It's like everyone's treating him and Ava like they're still in some crime documentary."

"Which, to be fair, they kind of are," Carly murmured, handing me a cold can of light beer from the cooler. "There's this one lady by the boardwalk hot dog stand who was talking loudly enough for everyone to hear, saying Ava was spotted yelling at Liz the day before she died. Full-on meltdown. She swore she saw Bauer standing there just watching, furious at the way Liz was treating 'his girl.'"

"Oof," I said, cracking the can open. "People are going to run with anything now."

"Tell me about it," Olivia said. "A guy at the hardware store was telling my dad that Ava was confidently back to heavily promoting The Shore Thing. The line outside was insane, a stir of people trying to buy stuff just to 'get a read' on her vibe. Like they'll spot a murderer by how she rings up stuff and insert themselves into the investigation."

Carly smirked, leaning back on her elbows. "I went by to peek. Can confirm: Ava looked *pissed.*"

I stretched my legs out, watching the tide roll in. "How pissed?"

"Like . . . loudly snapping at Bauer in front of customers while they were stocking the store, pissed," Carly said, raising her brows. "And guess who was there? Like always."

"Adam," I sighed.

"Adam," she echoed. "Hovering. He was practically glued to Bauer's side, talking to him like he was made of cracked glass. And then he starts bringing up old block party memories to 'keep Bauer's mind off everything.'" She air-quoted dramatically. "Stuff that made zero sense in the moment. Way too personal. Way too forward."

I stayed quiet for a moment, the sound of waves filling the gap. My mind flashed back to Bauer's drunken bar conversation, Adam's probing questions, and now the image of him hanging around The Shore Thing like some loyal watchdog.

Carly nudged my knee with her foot. "Earth to Claire. Don't go all Nancy Drew on us right now."

I forced a smile. "No promises."

TWENTY-SIX

Coral Haven felt like it was holding its breath.

Not in the storm-clouds-and-rain way, but in that strange, uneasy way. Even the gulls were quieter, circling the boardwalk with tired, lazy arcs instead of their usual squawking chaos.

I walked toward The Driftwood for my shift, sandals slapping the worn wooden planks. My pink Razr buzzed every few minutes with messages: Carly asking if I'd heard any updates, Olivia relaying gossip from her summer schoolteacher coworkers, even a few blog readers sliding into my inbox with important case information. It was almost too much noise, and yet I wanted all of it.

My inbox had turned into a circus.

The line between truth and rumor was already thin, but now it felt nonexistent. Everyone had an opinion about Liz's death, and apparently, they all thought I needed to hear it. My blog comments and messages were a disaster. Half condolences, half conspiracy theories written in all caps and riddled with typos.

One person swore Liz had been poisoned through a syringe, "a tiny pinprick during store hours," they wrote, claiming she'd been tangled up in a coke deal gone wrong. Another message spun a whole soap-opera scene about a long-lost sister, supposedly presumed dead, who had resurfaced to claim Liz's life insurance and The Sand Dollar's profits. According to that one, she'd hired an assassin to do the dirty work, making it look like a slow, unassuming death.

It was . . . a lot.

Most days I couldn't tell where the truth stopped and the delusions began. Still, part of me couldn't help reading every message, chasing the impossible thought that maybe one of them wasn't entirely off base.

As I turned onto the main strip, I involuntarily slumped.

The Sand Dollar was still abandoned, its windows dark and dusty. Across the street, The Shore Thing was very much alive, customers spilling out with bags of stuff from the store.

Bauer stood at the porch railing, his arms crossed and expression unreadable. Ava was inside, moving through the displays with a little too much energy, like she had something to prove.

I noticed Adam. He wasn't with them, not exactly. But he lingered. He was leaning against a lamppost, sipping from a Styrofoam coffee cup, eyes fixed on the boutique activity like it was a movie he didn't want to miss. When Bauer caught sight of him, he gave a slight nod. Adam smiled and turned his head. His gaze slid to me. He smirked, tipped his coffee like a toast, and strolled casually down the street.

By the time I reached The Driftwood, I already knew what tonight's blog entry would be. Not just whispers, and not just rumors. If Coral Haven had taught me anything, it was that the people who looked like background characters were often the ones with the darkest stories.

*

This Week on the Dunes: Farewells, Finger-Pointing & Far Too Many Emails

Saying Goodbye
Liz's funeral service is scheduled for Saturday afternoon at Our Lady of the Sea, with a reception to follow at the town hall. Expect the entire community to be there—both to mourn and, let's be honest, to watch who sits where and who doesn't show at all. In Coral Haven, funerals aren't just about grief; they're about reading between the lines.

Inbox Overflow
On a lighter note (or darker, depending how you see it), I should probably set up a filter for my messages. Ever since Liz's passing, my inbox has been flooded with anonymous tips, gossip, and more than a few attempts at framing ex-boyfriends, scorned lovers, and rival shop owners. One local wrote, "Check into the guy who sells the driftwood frames—he always hated Liz's candle displays." Another message blamed "an old high school enemy with unfinished business." And let's not forget the reader who sent three paragraphs accusing her yoga/Pilates instructor.

For now, consider me your inbox filter: I'll keep what's useful, toss the crazy, and bring you the stories worth watching.

Stay tuned, Beach Street readers. This mystery is far from solved.

—Claire Bear

TWENTY-SEVEN

Birds filled the air with noise, carrying on like death hadn't just settled into the town.

The morning of Liz Carper's funeral seemed far too lovely for mourning. Coral Haven's sky stretched wide and blue, the air sticky with salt and sea, but Our Lady of the Sea Chapel was draped in white lilies. The sweet, cloying scent of flowers tangled with the faint tang of ocean air, and for once, Beach Street was eerily quiet.

The timing of the funeral felt strange. *Late*, even. Weeks had passed since Liz's death, enough time for the shock to harden into something dull. I didn't understand how there could even be an open casket after all that time. I'd assumed Liz would have been cremated by now. Later I learned that in cases of suspicious deaths, a body can be held by forensics for four to six weeks. The morgue keeps it cold enough to stall the natural process. An awful, clinical kind of preservation. I hear myself and realize I'm overexplaining again. When things get uncomfortable, I hide in the details.

Earlier, Carly, Olivia, Madison, and I contemplated in front of buckets of fresh blooms at the florist, debating colors the way we might've once debated outfits for a night out. In the end, we agreed on a bright, cheerful arrangement of roses, lilies, and wild greenery. Something more like a celebration of Liz's spirit than a symbol of grief. When we carried it to the counter together, our hands brushed, and we shared a quiet smile. It was a small thing, but it was genuine.

*

It seemed as if everyone in town showed up at the church. Shop owners closed early, parents dressed squirming kids in pressed Brooks Brothers polos and khaki pants, and even the tourists hovered respectfully at the chapel's stone wall, whispering like they wanted to be part of the story but knew they didn't belong.

The moment I stepped through the heavy double doors of Our Lady of the Sea, the ambiance was quiet, solemn. The church had stood on the edge of town for generations, a Gothic silhouette against the uneven bricks lining the street, and inside it felt like time itself slowed down to a crawl.

Dark wood lined every surface. The pews, the pulpit, even the narrow beams that arched high above, disappearing into shadow. The ceiling seemed impossibly tall, drawing your eyes upward whether you wanted to look or not. The stained-glass windows poured jeweled purple-and-blue light across the stone floor, shards of sapphire and ruby spilling over rows of bowed heads.

The scent of old incense clung to the walls, faint but comforting, threaded with saltiness that always found its way in from the ocean. The sound of soft hymns echoed through the vaulted space, voices rising and falling like the waves

The pews overflowed. Liz's homemade candles burned along the altar, sending ribbons of coconut, linen, and lavender through the still air. The scent was soft but relentless, a reminder of her that attached to everyone's clothes. It almost felt like she'd planned it herself, organizing her own farewell.

The line to the casket clambered all the way down the aisle, slow and quiet, everyone moving like they were afraid to break the spell of the room. I took my place near the back of the greeting line and let my eyes stroll over the collage boards set up along the way.

Photos of Liz at every stage of her life filled them. Liz with a surfboard balanced on her hip, Liz laughing behind the counter at The Sand Dollar, Liz and her mom holding up seashell necklaces, both smiling like they shared a secret, and some photos that Bauer was obviously cut out of. Someone had tucked a handful of dried wildflowers into the corner of one frame; another had a ribbon pinned across the top that read *Our Sunshine*.

The closer I got to the front, the gloomier the mood grew. Candlelight flickered across the mahogany casket, a deep, rich wood. The line crept forward in solemn inches, people whispering condolences, sniffles echoing softly between hymns.

Liz's parents stood near the casket, their hands clasped together so tightly it looked painful. Her mother's face was pale and distant, eyes heavy-lidded. She had the very vacant calm of someone floating through the fog of Xanax and grief. Her father's eyes were swollen nearly shut, his skin blotched red and pink from days of crying. They looked hollowed out, two people trying to stand upright in the wreckage of their world.

When it was my turn, I stepped up, my palms slick against each other. "I'm so sorry for your loss," I said quietly.

Her father nodded once, his jaw trembling. Liz had his eyes, that same almond shape that always made her look like she was laughing, even when she wasn't. She also had the same sharp, determined line of her chin.

Her mother's hand found mine briefly, soft and cold, trembling like paper in the wind. Up close, it was impossible not to see Liz in her: the delicate slope of her nose, the frame of her shoulders, the way her mouth trembled when she tried to be strong.

"She . . . she loved this town," her mother whispered.

"I know," I said, my throat dry. "We all loved her. She was a wonderful person."

They gave faint, brittle smiles before turning robotic, exhausted . . . greeting the next couple waiting behind me.

I stepped toward the casket, my heart thudding in my ears.

Liz lay perfectly still, dressed in a pale blue gown that caught the light like faded glass. The lace along the collar and sleeves looked fragile, almost too delicate for the sunken body beneath it. Someone had smoothed her hair so carefully, every strand tucked into place, the single pearl clip glinting like a tear that had dried there. Her waxy figure displayed an unfamiliar sheen of death. Her skin had darkened slightly, her lips pressed too neatly together, her eyes sealed beneath faint brushstrokes of shadow.

Lining the inside of the casket were little treasures from her world: a string of tiny shells, a vial of sand, a few of her shop's pearls, and a folded note tucked beneath her hands. I didn't know what it said, and maybe that was for the best.

"Goodbye, Liz," I whispered, my voice barely audible over the soft organ that floated through the church.

I remained with her for only a moment longer before stepping aside to let the next mourner through. My chest ached, hollow. Liz had always been so full of movement, of drive, of quiet intensity.

Carly sat with her hands folded tight in her lap, her bottom lip trembling, eyes glassy but refusing to spill. Madison, ever the caretaker, had a tissue clutched so tightly it shredded between her fingers. Olivia leaned forward, elbows on her knees, staring at the altar like she could find some kind of answer in the candles' flicker.

No one spoke.

I reached for Carly's hand, giving it a small squeeze. She looked at me briefly and nodded, her mouth twitching in a sad attempt at a smile.

The four of us sat silently, black dresses clinging to our sunburned shoulders, eyes darting across the crowded room. Carly's fingers twisted and crumpled a tissue. Madison's mascara had left faint half-moons beneath her eyes. Olivia just stared ahead, expression blank, as the choir began another hymn.

Bauer sat near the front, his shoulders hunched, suit jacket too big on his frame, like he'd borrowed it at the last minute. Bauer had lost a noticeable amount of weight in the last weeks, his face gaunt and pale. He didn't cry, but the hollowness in his face made him look decades older. Ava sat stiffly at his side, flawless as always in a sleek black sheath dress, her golden hair twisted into a perfect knot. Her black oval sunglasses stayed on through the entire service, even indoors, like a shield. Bauer's parents were sitting next to both him and Ava, consistently consoling Bauer throughout the ceremony. Behind them, Adam leaned toward the aisle, not family-close but not too far either. His parents on either side of him, quietly mourning.

The whispers started before the priest even finished.

"Did you see Bauer's face?"

"Why is Ava acting like a victim?"

"Did anyone see the detective lingering around, staring at each of our faces? Basically trying to squeeze some sort of confession out of one of us. How ridiculously insensitive."

*

We all exited the church, following the instructions of the priest. People began to cluster in little tight-knit groups across the church lawn, some crying quietly, some already trading gossip in hushed tones. As the final hymn faded into the breeze, the crowd on the chapel lawn began to stir of sympathy, quiet sobs, the soft rustle of Kleenex tissues and dresses brushing against the grass.

Liz's parents stood near the front of the crowd close to Detective Hensley, clutching each other's hands as if letting go might undo them entirely. Her mother's face was pale and raw, eyes rimmed red, while her father's jaw trembled as he tried to keep himself composed. The grief between them was bottomless.

Detective Hensley stood straight, arms folded, speaking quietly to an officer as the hearse idled down the block.

When the pastor finished his closing prayer, Liz's father stepped forward, his voice shaking as he addressed the gathered crowd.

"Please," he said, the single word cutting through the hush. "If anyone knows *anything* . . . even the smallest thing . . . please come forward to the police. Our Liz didn't deserve this." His throat caught, and his wife laid a trembling hand against his arm. "Please, I'm begging you. Someone out there knows what happened. We just want the truth. We want our Lizzie to get justice and peace. Please, please." He sounded defeated.

The silence that followed was absolute. A few people nodded through their tears. Others reached for their loved ones.

As I scanned the crowd, what struck me wasn't Ava, or even Bauer. It was Carly. My friend, my Pilates-loving, always-cheerful Carly. At one point, when Bauer stood to hug a cousin, I noticed her expression stiffen, and it did not include the empathy we all had. Just for a second. Maybe I imagined it. Maybe it was nothing. But it lodged in my brain like a splinter.

"Half the town was staring at Ava," Carly murmured beside me, slipping on her sunglasses. "Like they expected her to confess right there on the altar."

"Or Bauer," Olivia added. "No one can decide who looks guiltier."

*

In between the funeral and reception, I decided to make an impromptu blog post using my phone's internet browser to keep our little, intrusive, curious town updated.

*

This Week on the Dunes: Special Edition. A Farewell to Liz

Sunlight and Lilies
Liz Carper's funeral service at Our Lady of the Sea was beautiful. Painful, yes, but beautiful. The pews overflowed with locals, shop owners, and families dressed in their best, while Liz's own signature candles flickered along the altar. The whole chapel smelled like lavender and linen—a little detail that made the sendoff feel uniquely hers.

The Whispers
Of course, even grief in Coral Haven comes with a side of gossip. We said goodbye to Liz, but the story isn't over. The whispers are growing louder, and I can't help but wonder which ones are smoke . . . and which ones are fire.

—Claire Bear

*

The funeral reception at town hall had barely ended when my cell buzzed.

"Claire, it's Detective Hensley."

Her voice was brisk but not unfriendly, like a teacher calling you after class. "I'd like you to come by the station. Tonight, if possible."

My pulse jumped. "Yeah, I think so. I don't have a shift and no babysitting tonight. Did something happen?"

"Nothing new to announce," she said carefully. "But we need to compare notes. I have an instinct you've been collecting information." A pause. "And I think it's time we share. I must be missing something here."

*

The station was quiet when I arrived, the kind of hush that felt uncomfortable, like it had settled into the walls.

Detective Hensley waved me in from her office doorway. "Come on in, Claire."

Her office was smaller than I expected, tight and windowless. But what struck me immediately was how *neat* it was. Every file was squared at perfect angles, every pen lined up beside a notepad, a fresh cup of coffee placed precisely in the center of a coaster. Even the blinds were leveled so evenly they could've been measured with a ruler. The woman radiated boss ass bitch, and her workspace matched it.

Except for one wall.

A corkboard dominated the space behind her desk. It being messy, layered, and almost obsessive. Photographs and notes overlapped in a collage of tragedy and theory. Red string linked corners of the board like veins in a body.

My gaze skimmed across the details, absorbing more than I probably should have.

There was a hospital bracelet, looped over a thumbtack, with *Elizabeth Carper* written across it in smudged ink and dated one week before her death.

Pinned beside it were photos—Liz smiling behind the counter at The Sand Dollar, Bauer caught scowling mid-conversation outside his boutique, Ava standing stiffly near a display table, her expression unreadable.

But then something else caught my eye, someone I didn't recognize.

A blurry security camera photo, timestamped sometime during the week of Liz's death, showed a UPS delivery driver carrying a long, rectangular box toward the shop. His face was half-obscured by the brim of his cap, but the size of the package caught my attention—narrow and compartmental-looking.

Confusing. Interesting.

"Alright," she began, folding her hands on the desk. "You've been blogging, talking, listening. Normally, I'd tell someone in your position to back off. But in this case, people are talking to you way more than they are to me. They trust you. So, I need to know what you've heard. Or rather, I'd be very appreciative if you'd divulge the info you've been collecting. I'm at a loss and need to think outside the box."

"This isn't standard procedure," Hensley added, as if reading my thoughts. "But Coral Haven doesn't have the manpower for blind spots, and right now, unofficial help has become a necessity."

For a brief second, I thought about lying. Or at least, leaving certain names out. Omitting speculations. Carly's, especially. She was my friend, one of my closest, and even though her behavior at the funeral had confused and thrown me, it felt like a betrayal to bring her into this room, under this kind of light. But then I thought about Liz. The flowers on her casket, the way her mother's hands had trembled during the service. If I kept quiet and it turned out Carly, or anyone, knew something important, I'd never forgive myself. I wasn't a detective, but I wasn't blind either. And Liz deserved honesty.

I swallowed, then nodded. "Okay. At the funeral, there were whispers about Ava. That she was too polished, too cold. And Bauer looked . . ." I hesitated, thinking of his hollow face. "Destroyed. Like he'd already lost everything. His demeanor has changed drastically."

"Okay. Noted. And?"

"And Adam was there. Watching Bauer. Not the processional for Liz. Just Bauer." I shifted in my seat. "It unsettled me. And my friend Carly—" I stopped. "She looked at Bauer in a way that didn't feel . . . normal. Sharp. Like anger, resentment. I don't know if it means anything, but I want to cover my bases. I know there might be zero connection whatsoever, sorry."

Hensley jotted something down, her pen tapping quickly against the page. Then she continued, "Okay. Okay. Good. That matches some of what I've heard. It seems like Carly and Liz may have had a business or personal dispute last year. This isn't confirmed. Small, but potentially relevant."

I kept my face expressionless, but inside, my thoughts slammed into each other.

Carly and Liz? Bad enough to be noted?

That didn't sit right. Sure. Carly was . . . blunt, sarcastic, opinionated, sharp when she needed to be. But secretive? Calculated? Dangerous? No. The idea felt wrong in my body, like a truth bent just enough to make me uneasy

"As for Adam Morgan—" Hensley's eyes flicked up to mine. "He's on my radar too. No priors, but he circles Bauer like a moth to a flame. I just haven't found anything concrete. I'm starting to become curious about their relationship. It seems very one-sided."

That part, at least, made sense.

Then she leaned back. "Here's the deal, Claire. I need you to keep listening. Keep writing if you must, but filter what you put out there. Don't post anything that could spook the killer, or we'll lose our chance. Share it with me first. Clear?"

I exhaled, and tension coiled in my chest. "Clear."

"Good." She closed her notebook, eyes steady on mine. "Because whoever poisoned Liz knew her well enough to get close. To make her trust them. And that means they're still close. To you. To this town. Maybe even to me."

A shiver crawled down my spine.

It didn't feel like I was just writing a blog. I was hunting a killer.

TWENTY-EIGHT

"Work for those *big booties*, girls!"

Rows of reformers and mats stretched across the polished wood floor, each one occupied, every breath in sync with the steady rhythm of my friend's voice.

At the front of the room stood Carly. She was poised, confident, and radiating a calm authority that made twenty-odd strangers trust her with their bodies. She counted out cues with crisp precision, her tone encouraging but firm, as though she willed everyone in the room to find just a little more strength, one more controlled breath. Sweat glistened on foreheads and arms, the collective effort rising like a tide.

Some participants moved with practiced grace, their cores steady and movements exact, while others wavered slightly, wobbling through the harder holds, stealing glances at the clock only to find they still had half the class left. Yet no one dropped out; the energy was too high, the camaraderie too binding.

By the end, my legs felt like linguine and my tank was sticking in all the wrong places. Madison was doubled over, pretending to stretch but just wheezing, while Olivia had already whipped out her phone to snap a post-workout picture.

"You look like a tomato," she told me, grinning as she adjusted her high ponytail.

"That's because I *am* a tomato," I gasped. "A tomato that needs a mimosa. A.k.a. champagne, one drop of orange juice."

"Good thing it's No Shower Happy Hour," Carly said, tugging her tank top into place. "Straight from sweat to sand. No judgment, no makeup, just booze, girlies. We worked for those calories!"

The four of us stiffly shuffled toward the outside/inside beach bar, our sneakers kicking up sand, endorphins making us a little too giddy.

Which made it the perfect time.

"So," I started, lowering my voice just a notch. "I have to tell you something. But you need to promise not to freak out. Seriously."

Madison squinted. "You're pregnant . . . Wait no, you got bangs, or your Brazilian wax went awfully wrong. Don't worry, we'll support you."

"No," I said, rolling my eyes. "It's about the case. About Liz."

That got their attention. Carly slowly rolled her eyes, having had enough of these conversations. Olivia stopped mid-uploading, and Madison straightened her spine.

"Detective Hensley called me in last night," I said. "We talked. She wants me to keep listening, to keep writing. But she asked me to share what I find with her first. It's kind of an alliance."

"Wait—" Olivia blinked. "You're like . . . the detective's sidekick now?"

"Not a sidekick," I corrected quickly. "More like her civilian source."

Madison let out a dramatic gasp. "You're going to end up murdered in chapter forty-seven, you know that, right?"

Carly elbowed her. "Don't joke." But her tone was flat, her expression unreadable.

I filed it away. Carly again. A flicker, nothing more. But still.

"Anyway," I said, forcing a smile. "If anyone knows anything. Hears anything. Tell me first, okay? We can filter it before it becomes blog fodder."

"Girl detective," Olivia sang, slinging an arm around my shoulders. "Now let's go get more drinks, I want to be plastered. Today is my day, ladies, I'm feeling it."

We stumbled for more drinks, looking like absolute chaos among the neatly dressed tourists. And for a fleeting moment, all that mattered was friendship.

But the salt air and the sound of waves couldn't quite drown out Detective Hensley's words from our conversation.

Whoever poisoned Liz is still close. To you. To this town.

TWENTY-NINE

It was lively on the strip (duh), heat-exhausted tourists and locals mingling under the big plastic umbrellas. The bar sat just off the sand, painted a bright orange, its weathered wooden deck half-shaded by wide umbrellas that flapped lazily in the breeze. A small band made up of guitars, a steel drum, and a singer with a voice roughened by drugs and cigarettes had filled the humid afternoon with music that begged for bare feet and easy smiles. Their rhythm carried across the beach, drawing in tourists like gulls to a scattering of fries.

Some people leaned on the railings, nodding along to the beat, while others let themselves be pulled onto the sandy edge of a makeshift dance floor. A drunk couple danced, cheeks shining red, Hawaiian shirts too dumb, twirling clumsily to the music, laughter spilling from them. Teenagers filmed short, shaky clips with their digital cameras, trying to capture the fun to upload later when Wi-Fi was a luxury. Every face seemed loose, freer.

Carly was already at the counter, charming the bartender into doubling her lime wedges, while Madison and Liv and I grabbed a new spot closer to the band at a high-top table overlooking the sand.

I waited until Carly had wandered off toward the patio with a margarita in one hand, chips and guac in the other. I leaned into Madison.

"Okay," I said quietly, twisting the paper wrapper off my straw. "I feel like an awful friend, but be honest with me. Has Carly ever had . . . issues with Liz?"

Madison blinked. "Like, Pilates studio drama?"

"No. Like actual beef. I saw something weird and didn't know if it meant anything. The way she looked at Bauer during the funeral—" I lowered my voice. "It felt personal."

Olivia exchanged a glance with Madison, then leaned closer. "I mean, you don't know the whole backstory, do you?"

I stared at her, confused. "What backstory?"

"Carly dated Bauer," Madison whispered, eyes wide like she couldn't believe she was saying it out loud. "Right before Liz did. It was a whole thing. And Carly and Liz were in rival friend groups in high school—you know, the cheerleaders versus the volleyball girls. Classic Coral Haven drama."

I nearly choked on my margarita. "Wait. Carly dated Bauer?"

"Briefly," Olivia said quickly. "Like, months. But still. Then Liz swooped in, and the two groups basically froze each other out for a whole year. But come on, that was forever ago."

"High school forever ago," Madison added, popping a chip into her mouth. "Which, in this town, is practically yesterday."

I glanced toward the patio, where Carly was laughing with another group, sunlight catching the edge of her gold hoops. My best friend, the one who dragged me to boot camp, who brought me coffee every Monday, who knew my shit before I did.

And suddenly, there was a tiny fracture in the picture I'd painted of her. A sliver of doubt I hadn't expected.

Because sure, the drama was ancient history. But was it actually?

THIRTY

The longer Liz's case went unsolved, the louder Coral Haven became.

Anywhere you ventured in town, you couldn't escape it; news was still teeming with killer and murder theories. The community could not believe Liz's case wasn't solved yet. Everyone had a theory—the barista at The Beach Babe, the lifeguards, the woman who sold beef jerky on the boardwalk. People were getting annoyed with how the investigation was being carried out.

Carly had her elbows on the counter one afternoon, flipping through the local paper. "It's almost like people are trying to *manifest* the killer," she said. "Half these stories contradict each other."

Olivia leaned in. "My favorite so far? Someone swears Liz was seeing a man who wasn't from town. A tourist. Tall, dark, handsome, mysterious, drove a truck.

Supposedly came in and out of The Sand Dollar late at night."

Madison made a face. "Or someone just saw a UPS guy."

"No, seriously," Olivia insisted. "My neighbor said her elderly mom saw him. It was around closing time, right before Liz died."

Carly tapped her nails on the counter. "Could be anyone. It could be *anyone*. A fling gone bad, a jealous girl, a stalker. If she was seeing someone from out of town, it'd be a nightmare for the police to trace."

"Or family," Madison said quietly. "Remember how Liz never really talked about hers? She's lived here forever, but I never met her parents until her funeral. What if there's bad blood there? Money, inheritance, something deeper?"

We all fell silent at that.

It was strange. They'd all known Liz for years, yet none of us really *knew* her.

Beneath her immaculate boutique displays and her polite smile, there were pieces of her life that were completely off-limits.

A secret relationship, a vengeful relative, a delivery man, a stranger who will disappear after summer's end. It wasn't impossible.

I jotted a few notes on a napkin while they talked, not as gossip this time, but as something that might matter later. Because if the rumor mill was churning this hard, at least one of those whispers had to come from a grain of truth.

*

I curled on the couch with my laptop, opened a blank document, and started typing notes like I was sketching out suspects for one of those true crime books.

I hesitated to begin and then slowly started typing.

Carly. Am I making a mole out of a molehill? My best friend. The one who dated Bauer before Liz. Rival friend groups, leftover tension, that flicker of something sharp at the funeral.

I didn't know exactly what had happened between Carly and Liz. Only noticed that there were moments when the air between them felt tight, conversations that ended a beat too early, smiles that didn't quite reach the eyes.

Was it possible Carly had used this shop drama and chaos as cover? Taken advantage of a town already primed to blame Bauer, Ava, anyone but her? Had she seen an opening and stepped through it, committing the perfect crime while everyone else was looking the other way?

Ava. The obvious choice. Too polished and cultured for town, too ambitious for Bauer, too angry at Liz. A reputation for cutting down anyone in her way. A mysterious dead coworker. But too obvious? Maybe that's why the whole town's gossip circle keeps landing on her—because she fits the role too perfectly.

Bauer. Broken. Drinking too much, wearing his guilt like an anchor. But what's the guilt *about*? Did he kill Liz in a fit of bitterness and regret? Did he kill Liz to make Ava truly believe he's devoted to her? Or did he still love Liz, and that's what's driving him into the bottle? He looks like a man who lost everything. But does losing someone and murdering someone look the same? The main motive for murder would be for his new store to flourish and become quickly financially successful. As well as keeping Ava happy. Liz did owe Bauer thousands of dollars, after all.

Unknown. Potential random suspect. Scorned lover? Uncovered truth with family drama? Town theories and rumors. Delivery guy? Someone mentioned seeing a UPS driver delivering packages to The Sand Dollar.

I chewed on my fingernail, staring at the half-finished list.

Adam. I typed his name and immediately backspaced it away. Too flimsy, too strange, too—what? Unsettling, yes. But nothing concrete. Not yet. He was a tad creepy, always trying to impress Bauer.

I closed the laptop with a sigh, stretching out on the couch.

Somewhere between the hanging weight of Liz's death and the endless stream of rumors, I realized my birthday was slowly creeping up. I hadn't even thought about it with everything going on. The last two years, the girls made a production out of it: a dinner on the boardwalk, a cake Carly somehow balanced on the handlebars of her bike, cocktails we had no business drinking in public. My birthday and the end of our town's summer season coincide, so the parties have been somewhat extravagant.

I'd have to ask them what the plan was this year. If there even was one. If there even should be one. But it would be nice to think about something other than suspects, funerals, and rat poison.

THIRTY-ONE

That night, I sat at my kitchen table with the glow of my laptop cutting through the dark. The words came slowly, haltingly, but they came. If I was going to be in this "alliance," then I needed to act like it. As I drew up my email for Hensley, I made an executive decision to remove Carly from any updates. My best friend, my investigation.

To: Detective Hensley
From: Claire Collins
Subject: Notes

Detective,

Here's what I've gathered lately, both from whispers and what I've seen myself:

- **Unknown** → I'm keeping this as a possibility. There are many outside factors that should be considered. A feud with a current love interest? A vengeful customer? There are rumors of Liz asking rambunctious tourists to leave her store.

- **Ava** → Cold and composed at the funeral. Known temper, ruthless ambition. The angry phone call the night before Liz died. Whispers that she has "a body" in her past—the accident at her last job. The town sees her as guilty.

- **Bauer** → Drinking heavily, looks hollowed out. Seems guilt-ridden, but unclear if it's grief or something darker. Still a potential suspect.

- **Adam** → . . . I hesitate to write this, but something about him unsettles me. HE IS SO WEIRD. The way he lingers and appears out of nowhere, the odd things he says. No proof, just instinct.

This might be nothing. But Madison told me Liz had been to the hospital earlier that week. Stomach pain, nausea. But there was a weird call afterward. It sounded like someone prying for Liz's patient information. Could be nothing.

That's what I've got for now. I'll keep listening.

—Claire

I hovered over the send button, heart racing, then finally clicked.

Her reply came faster than I expected.

From: Detective Natalie Hensley
To: Claire Collins
Subject: RE: Notes

Claire,

Thank you for your notes. They've been more helpful than you probably realize. Keep documenting *everything* you hear. Any direct quotes, names, times, locations, anything that could connect dots we might be missing.

Now, I need to make something absolutely clear.

What I'm about to share with you is *strictly confidential*. This does not leave this email. You cannot repeat, reference, or hint at it. Not on your blog, not to your friends, not even in passing conversation. If this leaks, it could compromise the entire case, and I'll have to officially remove you from any cooperation going forward. I'm trusting you because, frankly, I'm at a standstill and the people in this town are talking to you more than they are to me. And people are starting to get angry.

Here's where we are:

Two empty wine bottles were recovered from the crew area at the back of Liz's store, found in the trash during a second search. Both tested positive for traces of bromadiolone. This wasn't a single dose, whatever she ingested had been building in her system.

Each cork had a small puncture hole consistent with injections or contamination through what we assume was a syringe. We found a popped silver balloon behind the clerk counter, as well.

We were able to lift partial prints from the glass and corks. They are being processed now.

Given Ava's inconsistent statements, strong motive to eliminate Liz, and her previous connection to a workplace fatality at her former employer, Ava Delaney is at the top of our suspect list.

Again, Claire. This is not for your blog.

I'm telling you this because people trust you, and you have access to conversations I never will. I need you to keep listening, keep observing, and keep asking questions. Subtly, pointedly. Anything you hear that sounds off, I want it in my inbox immediately.

Be smart, Claire. You're walking a fine line here.

—Hensley

I stared at the screen, pulse thudding in my ears.

Ava. Two bottles. Motive. Poison. And a freaking balloon?

Moments after reading Hensley's email, my phone lit up with a familiar name on the caller ID just as I was about to shut my laptop for the night.

Mom.

I winced. Six missed calls blinked in the log. Guilt washed over me as I flipped to answer.

"Claire? Finally!" Her voice rushed through the line, equal parts relief and panic. "Do you know how many times I've tried you? I almost called the police myself."

I closed my eyes, pressing my forehead into my hand. "I'm sorry, Mom. Things have been . . . crazy."

"Crazy?" she echoed. "Honey, you told us about that Carper woman's fight with her fiancé—how ugly it got. And now she turns up poisoned, and nobody's been arrested? And you don't answer your phone? What am I supposed to think?"

I sank deeper into the couch, the shadows of my living room pressing close. "I know. I should've called."

"And don't get me wrong," she continued, steamrolling the apology, "your father and I are a little behind. The mail's been backed up ever since we got back from vacation, and we haven't exactly been glued to the news. But still, this is not the kind of update a mother wants to piece together."

"I'm still alive," I said softly. "I'm okay. I promise."

She didn't sound convinced. "What happened to that little blog of yours? Why can't you write about—oh, I don't know—recipes, or children's books, or literally anything that doesn't involve dead bodies?"

Despite everything, I smiled. "Because that's not Coral Haven this summer, Mom. People want answers."

"Answers should come from detectives and police," she said, her voice cracking now, gentler. "Not from my daughter."

"I'm already in the middle of it," I admitted quietly. Then, quicker, before she could interrupt: "But I'm careful. I swear."

There was a long silence, where I could picture her sitting at the kitchen counter back home, one hand wrapped around her mug, the other rubbing the bridge of her nose the way she always did when I stressed her out.

"Do you want me to drive down?" she asked finally. "Stay with you for a bit? I can be there by tomorrow."

My throat tightened. Part of me wanted to say yes. To let her swoop in, make casseroles, fill my fridge, and stand between me and every shadow in Coral Haven.

But I couldn't. Not with everything unraveling, not with secrets piling up that I couldn't explain.

"No, Mom. I'm okay. I promise. You don't need to worry."

"I'm your mother. Worrying is my job."

"I know." My voice softened. "And I love you. I'll call you every day, I swear."

A pause. Then, grudgingly: "Every day. Or I *will* drive down there."

I laughed, though my chest ached. "Deal. Goodnight, Mom."

When the call ended, I set my phone down and stared at the wall, the electricity of the refrigerator suddenly the only sound in the whole apartment. It was such a small noise, but somehow it made the silence feel so much louder.

For a moment, I wished I could crawl back into being someone's child again, when the worst thing that could happen was scraped knees or a bad grade, and comfort was as simple as my mom brushing hair out of my face.

But I wasn't that girl anymore. I was a grown woman who once dreamed of writing whimsical children's books and somehow ended up documenting murders in a beach town instead.

And Detective Hensley was counting on me—what I'd seen, what I knew, what I could give—to help close this case. I was not about to quit now.

THIRTY-TWO

I heard a sudden shriek through the noise, sharp enough to make me flinch. My heart lurched before I realized the source: A little boy bouncing on his toes in front of a claw machine, clutching a stuffed shark he won. Jesus, dramatic.

The boardwalk was packed, people with dripping ice cream cones weaving between lackadaisical groups, the arcade buzzing with neon and laughter. From the outside, you'd never know there was an active murder investigation happening.

I was back to my mundane summer routine, clocking shifts at The Driftwood, scribbling blog notes between errands, and babysitting for the Schmidt family. It was almost a relief to lose myself in the chaos of twins under five: sticky popsicles, fights over naptime, and their troubling fascination with the dog's water bowl.

At The Driftwood, things felt the same and different all at once. The blender shrieked, the espresso machine hissed, and my coworkers sang off-key while wiping down tables. But the conversations around me were snippy, full of sideways glints and lowered voices.

At table three, two older locals leaned in close, whispering about the police finding poisoned wine bottles. I was baffled that this information had made its way to our rumor hall already.

"I heard Ava's prints were all over them," one said with relish, like she'd personally uncovered the clue. "Mark my words—they'll have her in cuffs any day now."

My phone vibrated with a text from Detective Hensley:

Still processing evidence. No arrests yet. Stay alert.

I stared at the words, thumbs hovering. Finally, I replied:

Understood.

Before I could simmer on it, the bell over the door jingled and Olivia breezed in with Madison, all sunglasses and bright energy. Olivia waved like she owned the place, then slid onto a stool at the counter.

"Two things," she announced. "One: I need caffeine. Two: We need happy things to talk about. Three: Meaning birthday plans. Four: We're not letting this pass with you stuck at home in pajamas. This is the third end of season celebration we have together, Claire! Carly and I are already plotting," she said with an evil giggle.

Madison snorted behind Olivia. "That was four things, Liv. Plotting or scheming? Hey-hey!" she said while grabbing a seat.

"Semantics," Olivia said, grinning. She turned to me. "So, what do you want this year? Cake? Cocktails? Winery? Trip? Bowling? Bonfire on the beach? All the above?"

Their presence lightened the air, tugging me back toward something almost regular. We were laughing about who would sneak a piñata onto the boardwalk and debating the merits of margaritas versus sangria.

*

When my shift finally ended, I headed over to the beach, where Carly, Olivia, and Madison had staked out our usual patch of sand. Olivia had her giant striped umbrella jammed into the dune, Madison brought enough snacks to feed a football offensive line, and Carly stretched out in her bikini, trying to tan every inch of her body while covering her face with her yellow bucket hat.

Buckle in for another long cinematic description.

The sun was relentless, glittering across the waves. We always sat near the jetty, same spot every time, close enough to people-watch but far enough to avoid the families with screaming toddlers. The sand burned just enough to remind you that flip-flops were a survival tool, not an accessory. I had to keep my sunglasses on; the glare from the water was blinding, almost electric.

A few dolphins were playing close to shore, leaping through the surf, and everyone along the beach clapped and cheered as if we'd all been waiting just for them. Jet skis cut lazy figure eights beyond the breakers, their engines roaring against the crash of the waves, and every few minutes a small plane droned overhead, dragging a banner advertising happy hour specials or half-off brewery flights at one of the local bars. Our biggest concern was who'd be brave enough to wade into the surf to relieve themselves.

I watched Carly for a while, her hair fanned across her red towel, her laugh carrying over the crash of the water. She didn't look like someone carrying a murderous grudge. She looked like my best friend. Always the one who showed up with coffee on rough mornings, the one who got me out of my own head. The one who never judged our dumb actions.

And maybe I'd let the whispers about her and Bauer and Liz get too far. Maybe I'd let suspicion fill in the blanks. Playing detective was making me paranoid. Now, seeing her sprawled out in the sun, I knew. Whatever had happened a decade ago—some high school rivalry, a brief fling with Bauer—it didn't add up to poison and death. I realized I needed to reel in my amateur detective curiosity instead of suspecting everyone around me.

"Earth to Claire. Why are you staring at Carly like she's an alien?" Madison asked, crunching on twisted pretzels.

"I'm not," I said quickly, looking away. "Just . . . thinking."

Olivia smirked. "Okay, I've been thinking too. Thinking of more fun things. Thinking of things to look forward to. Thinking about how we're going to celebrate your birthday. Because we've decided it's happening whether you like it or not."

"Oh! Right, yeah," Madison said through a mouthful of pretzel. "And it's not gonna be some little dinner. We're talking *event.*"

Carly rolled onto her side, propping herself up on one elbow. "What are we talking about, girlies? Claire's birthday? That's forever from now! But, yes, she deserves a real party. A huge end-of-season bash. Big, huge, big, something memorable. Leave it to us," she rambled.

I laughed, shaking my head. "This seems outrageous. You guys are ridiculous."

But warmth spread through me anyway, curling in my chest. The shadows of Liz's death seemed far away.

We sprawled in the sand for hours, letting the tide creep closer and the sun burn our noses, talking about everything and nothing. Boys, bikinis, old summer flings, Olivia's never-ending feud with her landlord and her not-so-secret crush on Sean, the cook.

When the chatter died down, I concluded that Carly wasn't a suspect. I was an asshole. She was my best friend. I was delusional and too deep into this mystery.

And no rumor could convince me otherwise.

*

That night, I was munching on yogurt and a half-eaten banana—a single girl's delightful dinner—and not really watching a reality show rerun when my email pinged.

From: Detective Hensley
To: Claire Collins
Subject: Update

Claire,

I wanted to touch base with you directly rather than wait until our next meeting. Please keep this between us.

Confidentiality is a must right now, and I'm relying on you to keep this quiet.

We've been making progress. Some circumstantial evidence has begun to accumulate. I won't share all of it yet—partly because we're still verifying details, partly because it's dangerous to draw conclusions too early. But I will tell you this:

Our timeline is tightening. We're starting to see a clearer picture of Liz's final days, and who might have had access and the motive to harm her.

I know the gossip in Coral Haven is never-ending but remember speculation is not evidence. Stay careful about what you put in your blog. The wrong whisper in the wrong ear could make someone desperate.

I'll be in touch when I have more.

—Hensley

I read it twice, then a third time, chewing on my thumbnail. Circumstantial evidence. A clearer picture. She must be homing in on the killer.

The email left me restless, uneasy. I wanted answers, names, suspects I could pin down, not shadows and half-hints. But maybe that's all murder investigations were in the middle. Shadows and hints until something finally cracked open.

I closed my laptop, turned off the TV, threw out the remnants of food, and sat in the quiet of my apartment.

If Hensley was this careful with me, what else wasn't she saying?

*

This Week on the Dunes: After the Funeral, Life Goes On

A Remembrance Worthy of Liz
As mentioned in a previous post. If you were anywhere near Our Lady of the Sea, you know Coral Haven showed up for Liz Carper in the way only our town can. The chapel was overflowing with friends, neighbors, shopkeepers, and families, all carrying flowers so bright the altar looked like a midsummer garden. The stories shared about Liz were funny, heartfelt, and uniquely her—from her impeccable shop windows to the time she organized a last-minute candlelight vigil during a blackout. The grief was heavy, but the love was heavier. Liz was one of ours, and we said goodbye the way she deserved.

Now, a few brighter notes around town:

Tomato Festival at the Farmers' Market
Mark your calendars! Coral Haven's annual Tomato Festival kicks off this weekend. Expect juicy tastings, a salsa competition, and (if last year is any indication) a kid somewhere covered head-to-toe in marinara by noon.

Beach Tag Renewal Reminder
Planning to stick around for the rest of the season? Renew your beach tags this week for a discounted price. Your future self will thank you when you don't have to sprint down the sand trying to dodge the tag checkers.

A Sandwich Worth the Hype
Our local gluten-free restaurant, Seabreeze Eats, has debuted a new sandwich—roasted zucchini, basil pesto, and fresh mozzarella on house-baked bread. I've already tried it (twice) and let me tell you: worth every crumb.

And Yes, the Case
I know many of you are hungry for updates about Liz's case. I promise I'll continue to share what I can when it's responsible to do

so. Until then, let's hold on to the memory of Liz, take care of each other, and try to find joy in the little things—like fresh tomatoes and beach days.

See you on the dunes.

—Claire Bear

THIRTY-THREE

The boardwalk's biggest bar, The Breakwater, was pulsing during sunset. Lanterns swayed in the draft, fairy lights twisted up the posts, and the deck was packed shoulder-to-shoulder with a crowd of people, all clutching plastic cups of beer and cocktails that sweated with beads of humidity.

Our guy friends' band, Salty Lagoon, was halfway through their set. The bass line vibrating and pounding throughout the wooden shack. Olivia had dragged us straight to the front row, Carly was already dancing with another local friend group, and Madison and I were doing that awkward "half dance, half try not to spill our drinks" shuffle and snickering.

It was fun.

Then Madison froze, eyes wide. Her hand clamped around my arm.

"Don't look," she shushed, which of course made me immediately look.

Bauer and Ava had walked into The Breakwater.

They stood near the back of the deck, half in the shadows but noticeable enough that the whispers rippled quickly. Bauer stood out in the crowd. A tall guy with beach-tossed blond hair nearly touching his shoulders, surfer casual and effortless. His streetwear was sharp: designer sneakers, a crisp tee, and a jacket that looked quietly expensive; a sleek outfit that made people glance twice without knowing why.

Beside him, Ava was his perfect counterpart. Her long, wavy blond hair was styled with a precision that looked natural but wasn't, each lock catching the golden light of the setting sun. She dressed with an instinctive flair, her presence magnetic.

Together, they looked like they'd stepped out of a glossy photograph, impossible to miss against the laid-back backdrop of a local beach concert.

"Wow. They actually came out," Olivia said, leaning over, eyes wide.

"Woah, bold move," Carly muttered, tossing her hair as if daring anyone to say otherwise.

I watched them for a while. Ava smiled when someone greeted her, but it was awkward. Bauer laughed at something, but it came out too forced. It was obvious. They seemed strained and fragile but still tethered together by something that looked a lot like love. Or at least dependence.

Madison drained the last sip of her drink, wincing as the ice hit her lip. "Alright, ladies, we need another round.

Shots and drinks coming right up." She slid off her stool, weaving through the crowd toward the bar.

Carly whistled after her. "Make it tequila!"

The band launched into a cover that had the whole deck singing along, and when Madison finally returned, drinks precariously balanced in both hands, her eyes were wide with gossip and adrenaline.

She set the glasses down and leaned close, shouting, her voice just audible enough for me to hear over the music. "You won't believe what I just heard."

"What?" I couldn't help it; I sounded tipsy and eager.

"I went to grab us drinks," Madison said, swaying just a little as she talked, lowering her voice like it was a secret even though no one was listening. "And I walked right past them. Like—*right* past."

She paused, squinting like she was replaying it in her head. "Ava was whispering. I couldn't hear everything, but I caught enough. She said it was the *last* time she was going to talk about it. That Liz wasn't . . . totally innocent."

Madison shook her head, a little too emphatically. "She said they tried to make peace. Like, actually tried. But Liz refused. Just flat-out refused."

Then she leaned closer, breath warm and alcohol-heavy. "Apparently Liz wouldn't pay Bauer the money she owed him. And she was getting lawyers involved. Lawyers, Claire. Ava said she'd probably spend just as much fighting him as she owed in the first place, and blah blah blah."

She straightened, blinking at me. "Which is insane. Right?"

My stomach dipped. "And now . . . ?"

"And now," Madison said grimly, as she calculated the equation, "Liz is dead. No debt. No lawyers. No pressure."

The music swelled, the crowd cheered. On the far side of the deck, Bauer and Ava slipped away together, disappearing in the sea of people.

I stared after them, my warm drink in my hand, questions wrapping around my ribs.

If Ava was right, Liz hadn't just been an annoying victim. She'd been a huge problem.

And problems have a way of making people desperate.

*

Salty Lagoon wrapped up their final set to a roar of claps, woos, and whoops, and the deck unraveled into chaos. The good kind. Drinks were sloshed, flip-flops were lost, couples were grinding. Carly was spinning in a circle with one of the guitarists, hair wild, shrieking with laughter. Olivia was yelling something about cheese fries and trying to text a *You up?* to the cook from The Driftwood.

And I? I was drunk. Hammered. Like, drunk where your mouth works faster than your brain and your thoughts feel like they're covered in static and commotion. Wasted. Swaying.

Still, my eyes kept tracking Bauer and Ava. Ava in those impossible heels. Bauer moving like a storm cloud.

I stared after them, fuming.

I barely registered myself stepping away from my friends, the space between us widening with every angry stride. Someone said my name—maybe Carly, maybe Madison—but I didn't stop.

And then, like tequila-fueled bravery was pouring directly into my veins, I opened my stupid mouth.

"Hey, asshole!" I yelled, my voice shrieking. A few heads turned. "Remember when you cornered me on Beach Street? Said I wasn't a real local? That I was just some nosy blogger?"

Bauer paused, only slightly. But didn't turn around.

"Well guess what, dickhead?" I shouted, staggering half a step forward. "I am a permanent part of the town. Loser. And you're a murderous asshole with an anger issue!"

Someone near the bar gasped. The girls sprinted closer. Olivia tried to shush me with big, frantic eyes. Madison seemed about to throw her hand over my mouth, but decided against it.

"I wrote the truth, Bauer!" I kept going, my voice cracking with adrenaline. "Every word in my blog has been about finding the truth. So maybe you should be fucking careful!"

Bauer didn't even slow down. He just raised one hand over his shoulder and flashed the finger like a flag in the wind. No glance back.

I stood there, suddenly unsure if I was going to cry or puke or both.

And then, right on cue.

"Hey," a voice said behind me.

I whipped around, and there was Adam. Had he followed me? His red Solo cup in hand. That same mild, chipper, creepy smile.

"Great set, huh?" he asked. "Those guys always kill it."

I nodded, trying to steady myself. "Yeah. Killer."

He took a sip of his drink, eyes glancing toward the bar. "Bauer's still . . . well, Bauer, I guess."

I forced a smile, trying to pull myself back into a version of me that wasn't unraveling.

Adam leaned on the railing beside me. "You okay?"

"Totally," I lied. "Just needed air."

He nodded like he believed me.

"Don't stay out here alone too long," he said. "This town's been unpredictable lately."

Then he disappeared into the crowd, his words ringing after him like a warning.

THIRTY-FOUR

The sunlight stabbed through my blinds like punishment for mixing every kind of alcohol known to mankind. My head throbbed. My stomach lurched. I was sprawled on the tile floor next to my toilet, surrounded by a shrine of shame. Three different flavors of Gatorade (blue, red, and yellow, because apparently I couldn't decide which color would save me) and a small mountain of candy bar wrappers.

I'd also gone full feral at some point in the night.

Bits and pieces came back to me in nauseating flashes. The music, the dancing, Madison yelling "One more shot!" like a battle cry, and . . . oh God. Bauer.

I groaned, pressing an ice-pack to my forehead. What *did* I say to him? I remembered yelling. Loudly. Something about him being a "murderous asshole" and me being a "real local." My stomach twisted again. And not from the tequila.

By the time I made it to brunch, I was ten minutes late, wearing sunglasses and nursing a bottle of water like it was holy. The girls had already claimed our spot, right by the window, with the ocean glinting just beyond the boardwalk.

"You're not dead? Oh, wow terribly insensitive," Olivia said, waving a mimosa like a flag.

"Please," I groaned, sliding into my seat. "My body is ninety percent REGRET and alcohol."

Carly laughed. "I love you. Nice scene with Bauer last night. Olivia said you really told him who's boss. Madison has video. I could not stop cracking up."

"Delete it, don't show anyone," I said immediately with blushed cheeks.

"Absolutely not," Madison replied, grinning. "It's going in the archives."

A round of laughter broke out easily. I was happy the hangxiety was starting to leave. I easily won the contest of who had the worst hangover.

As the waitress refilled our water glasses, my mind flickered back to what I could remember from Madison's words last night—her whispered confession about what she'd overheard from Bauer and Ava. Liz owing money. Lawyers. A fight that might've pushed someone too far.

Between bites of my omelet, I said quietly, "I think I'm going to reach out to Detective Hensley later. Let her know what you heard, Madison."

Carly paused mid-sip. "What? What Mads overhead Ava talking about? About Liz and Bauer?"

"Yeah. If there was money involved, it's important. And if Ava was furious . . . that's motive territory," Olivia chimed in.

Madison frowned. "You really think they could've—"

"I don't know," I interrupted. "But Hensley should."

The conversation lulled for a moment; the only sound was the clink of silverware and the steady drone of brunch chatter around us. Then Olivia, our mood saver, clapped her hands together.

"Okay, enough detective talk, Claire. This is seriously depressing. We need to discuss something way more pressing."

I blinked. "Like what?"

"Your thirtieth birthday! Yay! Because we haven't planned anything. *Yet*," she said dramatically.

Carly perked up immediately. "After talking in circles the last time, we finally have a *list* of ideas. Ready?"

"Oh no, God help me," I muttered, but I was smiling.

Madison counted on her fingers. "Option one: a day on the boat. My stepdad is totally down to take us out. We could pack a cooler, play music, jump in the water—*classic Coral Haven chaos*. We'll anchor off the sandbar, get sunburned, and pretend the ocean isn't freezing."

Olivia leaned in, already animated. "And we could do the thing where everyone brings something homemade—like your mom's dip, Carly's weirdly good sangria, my guac that's basically a town legend. You know, some good old-fashioned debauchery at sea."

I snorted. "Until someone drops their phone overboard. Again."

"That was one time!" Madison said, laughing. "And technically it was your phone."

Olivia rolled her eyes. "Anyway. *Option two*—a barbecue at the park. Chill, good food, everyone brings something. We could set up near the dunes, string up lights, backyard games, maybe we can get the guys from Salty Lagoon to play if we bribe them with beer and girls."

Carly nodded enthusiastically. "Bonfire, s'mores, the works. We could invite half the town and still have room to dance. It'd be like an end-of-summer celebration. For you and for us surviving, well . . . all *this*."

Her tone softened slightly at that, the unspoken word *murder* hovering between us before Olivia cut back in with forced cheer:

"Option three," she said, wiggling her brows.

Carly propped forward abruptly and cut Olivia off mid-sentence, eyes bright. "Option three—and this one's my favorite. Adam's family winery. The inside venue would be free. We could dress up, do a private tasting, maybe rent out the patio. It's gorgeous at sunset."

I hesitated, picturing it: the golden light spilling over the vines, the sound of corks popping, laughter echoing off the hills. It sounded perfect. Serene and elegant and just far enough from the constant noise of the town.

"I actually love that idea," I admitted. "The winery. We haven't dressed up all summer, and I think this would be good for us. Something to really look forward too."

"Done," Carly said, clinking her glass against mine. "Claire's Coral Haven Birthday Bash: Winery Edition. I'll call Adam's parents tonight to reserve a day! Have you met them yet? They are so normal compared to Adam. I have no idea how that weirdo came from them."

Everyone tittered at that sly comment. The girls cheered, toasting me as if the idea were set in stone.

And maybe it was.

Somewhere, in the quiet between laughter and hangovers, I promised myself I'd text Detective Hensley later. I'd tell her about the overheard conversation, about the money, about the anger simmering beneath Bauer and Ava's smiles, and omit the part where I drunkenly confronted a suspect.

But for now, I let myself just be Claire, sitting and smiling with my best friends.

THIRTY-FIVE

That weekend, my phone was blowing up with notifications before I even had my coffee.

Carly: *Too excited to wait. Scouting winery trip today??*
Madison: *We deserve it.*
Me: *Already?! We just decided, guys.*
Olivia: *We're calling it research.*

The girls steamrolled and plans were made. Thirty minutes later, we piled into Carly's Jeep, windows down, our hair whipping in the wind as we went the four miles inland. The salty air gave way to warm earth and pine, and when we reached the Morgan Family Winery, the ocean breeze had turned soft and floral.

The vineyard stretched across gentle rolling hills. Rows of grapevines heavy with green fruit catching the sunlight like tiny glass beads. The tasting room sat at the top of the rise, a wide white building with ivy climbing its walls and large bulbs hanging from the wraparound porch.

Adam was waiting by the entrance, his hands shoved in his pockets, flashing that freaky, simple smile.

"You made it! Come on in," he said, voice warm. "Mom and Dad are inside and they're thrilled to help with your birthday plans. Especially with the added plus of our season officially ending."

Inside, the smell of both polished wood and fermenting fruit filtered around. Adam's parents, George and Jenna, greeted us with the kind of gracious enthusiasm that came from running a successful family business.

It struck me how much Adam resembled his mom. Jenna had that classic Mediterranean warmth. Olive skin that glowed even in the dim cellar light, dark hair that she'd pinned up in a neat twist, and deep brown eyes that seemed to take in everything. Adam had inherited all of it. His skin held that same sun-toned smoothness, his thick hair always a little tousled, like he'd just come back from the coast, and his eyes were rich espresso brown and had the same thoughtful calm as hers.

His father, George, was smaller, almost delicate in build, with wire-rimmed spectacles that kept slipping down the bridge of his nose. He looked more like a librarian than a winemaker. Gentle voice, careful movements, a man who probably alphabetized his wine bottles when no one was looking. Next to him, Adam seemed impossibly solid. He was taller, broader, and confident in that quiet way that came from being comfortable in your own skin.

"Claire, right?" Jenna asked, brushing her palms on her linen pants. "We heard you're our birthday girl!"

"Guilty," I said, laughing a little.

George ushered us toward a large chalkboard calendar on the tasting room wall. "Let's get you on the books before anyone else snags that weekend. Since it is the end of season." He flipped his marker cap off and neatly wrote *Claire's 30th Birthday – Private Event* in looping script across the date.

"Now," Jenna said, clasping her hands, "we'll handle the setup details. Tea lights across the patio, tables and tablecloths from storage, and, of course, a charcuterie spread that'll make you forget dinner exists."

"Wine," Olivia added, grinning. "Don't forget the most important part."

George chuckled. "Trust me, there'll be wine. Multiple reds, whites, and the summer rosé that's been flying off the shelves."

We followed them outside to the patio. The view rolled endlessly with vineyards fading into soft green hills, the faint silver line of the ocean glinting in the distance. It was breathtaking.

As we stepped out, I noticed Adam walking a beat behind his parents. There was a small but deliberate space between them; it was distance that wasn't accidental. His mother and father walked a step ahead, speaking quietly to each other, never quite looking back. Adam trailed them, hands shoved into the pockets of his jean shorts, his pink Morgan Family Winery shirt neatly pressed but somehow making him look younger, almost boyish. We followed the three of them into a separate area and arrived in an open courtyard with a table already full of wine flights.

"Let's begin the tasting!" Jenna said.

*

When we finally left, our shoes dusted with dry soil and our hair full of wind, we were tipsy and well-fed.

Carly dropped me off at home from our little recon mission and back at my bungalow the quiet settled around me like a soft blanket. The evening light filtered through the curtains, scattering across my desk where my notebook waited with half-filled pages of my newest children's story draft.

I picked up my pen and read what I'd written last week: *The little lighthouse who thought he was too small to shine.*

I smiled faintly and started sketching again, the story unfolding in soft pencil lines. But between paragraphs, my thoughts drifted back to Detective Hensley. Her last email, her clipped tone, the unspoken weight behind her words.

I needed to reach out soon. Maybe tomorrow.

I let myself imagine birthday lights flickering against the vines, laughter spilling into the night, and a town ready to celebrate the end of another season.

*

This Week on the Dunes: We're Gonna Need a Bigger Boat

If you've been feeling like Coral Haven's been a little wonky lately (I know I have), I've got some good news: The sunshine is sticking around and our town is soaking it up.

Winery Wanderings

A few of us took a spontaneous trip inland yesterday to check out the **Morgan Family Winery**—technically "research" for my very important upcoming birthday bash (yes, I'm milking it).

The place is stunning: rows and rows of sunlit vines rolling into the hills, the air smelling like fruit and oak. George and Jenna Morgan were absolute gems—they even offered to help set up for the party! Think twinkle lights, rustic tables, overflowing charcuterie boards, and their famous summer rosé.

It's the kind of place that makes you feel happy!

Community Fun Alert: "Jaws" on the Beach!

Mark your calendars: This Saturday at 7 p.m. the rec board is hosting a Movie on the Beach night! They're kicking things off with "Jaws." Because clearly, someone in planning has a sense of humor.

Bring a blanket, snacks, and your bravest friends (bonus points if you sit closest to the water). The town's setting up a huge projector, and vendors will be selling popcorn and sodas along the dunes. It's the perfect excuse to spend an evening under the stars, but don't let your feet dangle in the surf too long.

A Little Note . . .

It's been a rough summer. Losing Liz hit all of us hard, and I know there are still more questions than answers right now. The Coral Haven PD and Detective Hensley are continuing to work tirelessly on the case—and as always, I'll keep you updated when I can.

But for now, maybe it's okay to enjoy the good moments.

See you on the sand!

—Claire Bear

THIRTY-SIX

The morning sun was already spilling across my kitchen table when I opened my laptop. I took a sip of coffee, scrolled past new blog comments about the upcoming "*Jaws* on the Beach" event, and forced myself to focus on the one email I'd been putting off writing.

My fingers hovered over the keyboard for a long moment before I finally started typing.

To: Detective Hensley
From: Claire Collins
Subject: Some New Information

Hi Detective Hensley,

I wanted to share something that might be relevant to your investigation.

During the live concert at The Breakwater the other night, my friend Madison overheard a conversation between Bauer

Clips and Ava Delaney. It sounded tense. Ava mentioned Liz "wasn't as innocent as everyone thinks" and that there had been a serious disagreement over money. Apparently, Liz had refused to pay Bauer back after the business split and was threatening to get lawyers involved, something that could've cost him over ten thousand dollars.

I'm not sure what to make of it, but given everything, it didn't sound good.

Let me know if you'd like to talk in person.

Best,
Claire

I hit *Send* and immediately regretted it. Not because I didn't trust Hensley, but because once I'd shared that information, it wasn't mine anymore. It belonged to the case.

The reply came less than an hour later.

From: Detective Hensley
To: Claire Collins
Subject: Re: Some New Information

Claire,

Thank you for sending this along. Yes, I think it's best we meet in person to go over the details and make sure nothing gets lost in translation.

Can you do 4 p.m. today? There's a café called Pier Perk near the boardwalk. I'll grab us a table.

—Hensley

I exhaled, tension easing just a little. Meeting in person was better; there was less room for miscommunication, more chance to *read* her reaction. I was eagerly anticipating our meeting. But first, I had to get through a daunting morning shift.

The Driftwood was properly slammed that morning. The line snaked out the door, blenders whirred nonstop, and a kid spilled an entire smoothie across the pastry case. Wonderful. Between mopping floors, restocking napkins, and handing out espresso shots to hangry vacationers, the hours blurred together in a whirl of caffeine and chatter.

By the time my shift ended, I'd barely looked at the clock all day. My feet ached, my apron smelled like coffee grounds, and my nerves hummed with anticipation.

Using the employee bathroom at work, I changed into a clean beach cover-up, washed my face with sink water, tossed my hair into a bun, and headed down the boardwalk toward Pier Perk.

*

Pier Perk was busy but hushed, a mid-afternoon lull where the background playlist teemed, coffee machines whirred softly, and silverware clinked against ceramic. The air smelled like roasted beans and sugar.

Detective Hensley sat by the window, her gray blazer draped neatly over the chair beside her, a stack of folders and her badge resting just within reach. Her coffee was already half gone, the mark of someone who'd been there long enough to think.

I slid into the seat across from her. She gave a nod.

"Claire," she said. "Thanks for meeting me." Shaking my hand.

"Of course," I said. "I figured it'd be better to talk in person."

She flipped open a file, scanning a page before looking up. "What you mentioned in your email, about Bauer, Ava, and the money. It's useful context. Officially?" Her face tensed. "We're still concentrating on Ava, our prime suspect."

Hensley continued. "We can't get a solid alibi from her, Claire. Any one of the nights during the week of Liz's poisoning. Ava's fingerprints were found on both empty wine bottles retrieved from trash cans behind The Sand Dollar. Forensics confirmed traces of rat poison inside both bottles. We're still verifying the origin, but the bottles themselves came from Morgan Family Winery. Fairly common stock, but . . ." She exhaled slowly. "Still. The fingerprints are what concern us most. As well as her lack of straightforward alibi. We are still searching for the container or box the rat poison came from that would've been in her possession. No luck so far. As you know, we also found a popped silver balloon in the trash can behind the register. We're unsure if this is connected. This means we have means, motive, and opportunity."

I swallowed.

She stirred her aromatic coffee, her spoon tapping rhythmically. "We're also combing through security footage from the surrounding shops. Two of the cameras directly facing The Sand Dollar were non-functional. One was broken and the other disconnected weeks ago. We did recover footage from the bakery down the block, but it's grainy. The team's enhancing it now. Doesn't seem like it'll be useful though. Every avenue needs to be covered."

The surroundings of the café around us faded, and an uneasy punch in my gut hit hard.

"I know I already mentioned this in the email," I said, lowering my voice, "but it's been bothering me more the longer I sit with it."

Hensley waited.

"I told you that Madison overheard Ava telling Bauer that Liz wasn't innocent—that there was money owed, that lawyers were getting involved. What stuck with me wasn't the words so much as how heated it sounded. Not just angry. Defensive. Like Ava was trying to get ahead of something."

Hensley's gaze sharpened. "That fits with what we're seeing. If Liz was threatening legal action, that could've created pressure. And Ava . . ." She paused. "She strikes me as someone who doesn't handle pressure with grace, but with retaliation."

She jotted a note on the edge of her pad, then looked up again. "I appreciate you being forthcoming, Claire. These small pieces, even when they're gossip and rumors, sometimes push us toward a larger pattern. I need to reiterate the importance of your discretion. If this information leaks, a murderer may walk free."

I nodded, though the weight in my stomach didn't ease. "I just hope it helps. I keep thinking about Liz. She didn't deserve what happened."

"No one does," Hensley said, her tone softening quickly before hardening again. "We'll get answers. But I need you to stay observant. If Ava reaches out, if Bauer acts strange—anything at all, you let me know immediately."

I promised I would.

*

As I left Pier Perk, the sound of the waves just beyond the boardwalk blended with the murmur of tourists and the screech of gulls. But it all felt distant. The image of those wine bottles, the broken cameras, and Ava's face kept looping in my mind.

I walked home slowly, the late afternoon sun casting giant shadows across the boardwalk. My thoughts drifted, uninvited, to my upcoming birthday. To the vineyard, the laughter, the clinking of glasses under those pretty hanging lights.

The bottles came from Morgan Family Winery.

Adam's family winery.

For a moment, a chill fluttered through me, cutting through the warmth of the day. Was it just coincidence?

I pictured George's warm smile, Jenna's excitement as George wrote my name on their calendar. It couldn't be connected. It *shouldn't* be.

Still, a whisper of unease crept through my chest. Should I tell the girls we needed to pick a new venue? Just in case?

I shook my head as if to scatter the thought.

No. It wasn't important. Not now.

Besides, what could possibly go wrong?

What Happened to Liz

THIRTY-SEVEN

By dusk, the wind had picked up. It was that salty, restless kind of breeze that sent beach grass rustling and the scent of popcorn curling through the evening.

Half the town had already staked their spots along the sand, a patchwork sea of folding chairs, picnic blankets, and coolers. The parks and recreation board had rigged up a huge white backdrop between two poles with zip ties, which flapped gently as volunteers worked to anchor it down before the projector started. Strings of bulbs crisscrossed along the boardwalk and promenade, their soft glow spilling down over the crowd as families huddled together in sweatshirts, fuzzy blankets and beach towels.

My friends waved me over from a cluster of chairs near the lifeguard stand. Madison was already halfway through a bag of honey mustard flavored pretzels, Carly had a blanket wrapped around her shoulders like a cape, and Olivia was arguing with a friend-of-a-friend over which *Jaws* scene was the most iconic.

"You made it!" Carly called, lifting her drink.

"I had to stop for snacks," I said, hoisting a cooler onto the sand. "Priorities."

Olivia peeked inside. "Ooh, chips, grapes, and gummy sharks—thematic, very on brand."

"Obviously," I said with mocking seriousness. "If we're going to get fake-traumatized by a movie about sharks, we're doing it right."

People milled around us. Kids chasing glow sticks, couples walking barefoot along the surf, laughter rising and falling with the tide. Someone had set up a portable speaker, and "Under the Boardwalk" played faintly while the projector team tested sound. A few older couples began to sing along with the background music. The soft sounds lingering in the briny atmosphere.

When the lights finally dimmed and the ominous *dun-dun . . . dun-dun . . .* theme began to echo across the beach, a ripple of applause moved through the crowd. A couple of scattered children's screams hushed as the projector began.

As the movie played, the audience reacted like one big, living thing. There were gasps during the first shark attack, laughter at the dry one-liners and the cheesy dad jokes, and cheers when the scuba tank finally exploded the shark. The wind whipped harder toward the end, tugging at our blankets and hair, sending chips and popcorn rolling through the sand. But no one moved.

For two hours, no one talked about Liz, or rumors, or suspects. No one whispered about Ava or Bauer or the police.

When the credits rolled, the crowd clapped and cheered like the actors could somehow hear them. Parents gathered their kids, teens snapped selfies, and the faint buzz of conversation carried across the dunes.

Carly stretched and yawned. "That was perfect. Can we make this a weekly thing?"

"Only if next week's movie doesn't involve giant killing evil shark monsters," Olivia said. "I need at least one good night's sleep."

"You are an actual little baby, Liv," I answered.

We packed up our things slowly, dragging coolers and folding chairs back to the boardwalk under the golden haze of the streetlights. My cheeks hurt from smiling.

When I finally made it home, the house was quiet except for the rhythmic whisper of the tide outside my window. I washed the remnants of sand off my feet, slipped into comfy clothes, and collapsed onto the inviting couch with a sigh.

Detective Hensley and the Coral Haven police were on the job. The town was healing, finding little ways to come back to life. One movie, one laugh, one shared night at a time.

THIRTY-EIGHT

A sharp, loud ring jolted me out of sleep.

For a second, I had no idea where I was, just the shine of my bedside clock bleeding red across the room: 2:03 a.m.

My heart hammered. I fumbled for my cell phone, eyes still half-closed, sheets twisted around my legs. I'd been dead asleep, my brain on empty, and my body was refusing to move. My mouth felt dry, my eyelids grainy.

But the second I saw the caller ID—Detective Hensley—the fog burned away like steam. Adrenaline snapped through me, as strong as a double shot of espresso.

I flipped my phone open and pressed it to my ear. "Hello?"

Her voice, usually calm and measured, carried a rougher edge tonight.

"Claire," she said, "I apologize for the late call. We've confirmed a few things I think you'll want to hear."

I sat up straight, grabbing my notebook from the nightstand, my pen already uncapped. The tiredness was gone, replaced by that wired energy that always came before something big.

"Go ahead," I said, bracing myself.

"I remember you mentioning that Liz wasn't feeling well in the days before her death? Complaining about dizziness, fatigue?"

"Yeah," I said slowly. "From what I heard, she thought she had heat exhaustion or dehydration. She even closed The Sand Dollar early one day because of it."

Hensley exhaled through the phone. "Right. We pulled her hospital intake records from that visit. The ER staff logged her symptoms as dehydration and mild anemia. She was given fluids and sent home."

I frowned, already feeling the chill creep up my spine. "So, it wasn't dehydration?"

"No." The word landed abruptly. "The toxicology from her autopsy lines up with those same symptoms. Nausea, muscle weakness, confusion, all consistent with chronic exposure to small amounts of anticoagulant poison. We believe Liz ingested rat poison before the first time she was admitted, but it wasn't enough to kill her, frustrating the killer. She recovered, mostly. Then, a few nights later, she must have drank again. From the second bottle. That one had enough to stop her heart within hours."

I didn't realize I was holding my breath until I heard myself exhaling.

"So . . . in layman's terms, it was the wine," I murmured.

"Two bottles," Hensley said quietly. "Both from Morgan Family Winery. Forensics tested the wine sediment to create a timeline of when the tainted wine was ingested. One bottle opened days before her first hospital visit . . . the second, almost certainly the night she died."

I sat in silence, pen motionless above the page.

Hensley went on, her tone all business now. "That's how we're certain it wasn't accidental. It was deliberate. Premeditated. Whoever did this had access to both bottles and knew exactly what they were doing."

I swallowed. "Does this mean you're certain it was Ava?"

Hensley hesitated. "The evidence strongly points that way, Claire. Her fingerprints are the only ones on the bottles besides Liz's. And the pattern fits a poisoning method—it was planned, not impulsive. The cliché fits as well; poison is a woman's weapon, after all."

Her confidence should have been reassuring, but something about it unsettled me. It all seemed to line up too easily, like a cookie cutter crime novel. The timeline, the motive, the fingerprints.

"Thank you for letting me know," I said finally. "That . . . helps."

"Be careful, Claire," she said, her tone softening. "This is getting close to closing. People talk when they get scared."

After we hung up, I sat for a long time staring at the notes I'd scrawled:

Poison. Premeditated.

Outside, the wind rattled the shutters against my window. Spooky.

*

After hanging up with Detective Hensley, I couldn't shake the unease. I'd gone over her words again and again until they blurred together. *Deliberate, poisoned wine, Morgan Family Winery.*

There was no way I could fall back asleep after having that conversation. I powered on my laptop to draft a quick update for the blog. Something light, something to redirect my brain from the gravity of Liz's case. Maybe a small-town feature or an update on the beach cleanup schedule. But before I could start typing, I saw it.

A private message was waiting, unopened in my inbox.

No profile picture. No name. Just a generic gray icon and a timestamp from ten minutes ago.

From: Anonymous
To: Claire Bear
Subject: (None)

I think I know what happened to Liz.
I saw who delivered a balloon and wine bottles to her.

Meet me behind The Driftwood later, tonight @ 9:00pm.
Come alone

I reread it twice, my heart thudding. It didn't sound like a prank. No emoticons, no dramatic flair, just blunt, direct sentences.

I leaned back in my chair. The humdrum of the AC was the only sound in my apartment. Every instinct screamed that this was dangerous. But *what if* this was the break Detective Hensley needed?

Since it was still early morning, I had to wait for a respectable time to call my girls. Once it was appropriate, I grabbed my phone and called Madison. She picked up on the second ring.

"Hey! What's up? You never call this early."

"Can you add Carly? It's important. I know Liv is with her family, we'll catch her up later."

Within seconds, the three of us were on a scratchy three-way call, the sound of wind and distant static filling the pauses.

I word-vomited and explained everything. I told them about the message, the wording, the potential meeting behind The Driftwood.

"Oh my freaking God, Claire," Carly said immediately. "No. Absolutely not. That's how people end up *missing* in documentaries, murder stories, *Dateline*, the news?! You are basically pleading to be taken. We are not trained assassins, how are we going to save you?"

"Yeah," Madison agreed. "You're not meeting a random anonymous-ass person behind a bar at night. Like, duh? If they know where you work, that's already creepy enough."

"I know, I know," I said, rubbing my temple. "It's probably nothing. Maybe someone who wants attention or just playing a prank. But what if it's real? What if someone really saw something?"

"Then let the police handle it," Carly said sharply. "Send it to Detective Hensley. She'll set up the meeting, not you."

Madison's tone softened. "Claire, you've already done so much to help. You don't need to put yourself in danger."

I promised them I'd think about it. That I'd be smart. We hung up, and their warnings stayed in my mind.

But as I sat there, staring at that single gray icon on my screen, my curiosity began to gnaw at reason.

What if this was the one person who knew the truth?
What if they disappeared before anyone else could find them?

I closed my laptop slowly. In my head, I'd already decided.

I was going.

THIRTY-NINE

The message replayed in my head all day.
I saw who delivered a balloon and wine bottles to her.

It looped behind every customer's voice at The Driftwood, beneath the hiss of the espresso machine, even over the blast of the kitchen fan. I barely heard the talk about weekend specials or the low thump of the café playlist. My focus kept drifting to the clock.

8:02 p.m.

8:17.

8:28.

When my night shift finally ended at 8:30 p.m., I sprinted under the shine of the boardwalk lights, my thoughts deafening enough to drown out any other sound.

Madison and Carly's warnings echoed in my head, but this wasn't about curiosity anymore. Not really. It was about Liz. About finding something *real* in a mess of half-truths, gossip, and grief.

If someone truly saw who gave Liz those wine bottles, I couldn't ignore it.

I quickly arrived back in my apartment and hastily changed into something simple. Yoga pants, sneakers, a black zip-up hoodie. Practical. Quiet. Something I could easily flee in, if I needed to. I tucked my small canister of pepper spray into my pocket, slid my whistle onto my wrist like a bracelet, and double-checked that my phone was fully charged.

Nerves fluttered low in my stomach. Half adrenaline, half regret.

As I slipped out the door, the air had that coolness before a storm. Streetlights blinked against the mist rolling in from the ocean. The town looked softer at night, but also lonelier.

I arrived back at The Driftwood, its porch lights burning a tired amber. I stayed close to the sidewalk, scanning the edges of the alley that curved behind the building.

9:01 p.m.

I tightened my grip around my phone and walked into the shadows. Pepper spray readily accessible.

*

At first, I thought no one was there. I figured the message was some asshole fucking with me.

The back of The Driftwood was quiet. There were small creaks from the bar inside, the faint clatter of bottles being restocked. A dumpster sat under the flickering security light; the smell of salt, beer, and damp cardboard reeked in my nose.

Then I saw a figure.

Standing by the edge of the alley, half-lit by the streetlight, was a woman—short, rounded shoulders, a thin scarf around her neck, and a crown of unmistakable bright red hair.

She turned slightly, and my stomach lurched.

"Carol?" I said before I could stop myself.

Carol McKinney. Coral Haven's known resident oddball. She'd worked the counter at Seaside Bakery for as long as Carly has lived here (her whole life), the one who always remembered your usual order before you opened your mouth. She was known for her gossip but never mean-spirited about it. She had that kind of small-town curiosity that lived in everyone here, and I was guilty as well. We hadn't spoken much beyond morning pleasantries and the occasional coffee refill, but she'd always struck me as someone who saw everything and said nothing. A good, reliable source for information.

She blinked, startled—eyes wide like a deer caught in headlights. "Claire. You came."

I stepped closer, the gravel crunching beneath my sneakers. "You were the one who left that message?"

Carol nodded, her eyes darting past me, then over my shoulder toward the dark mouth of the alley. "I didn't know how else to reach you," she said in a low rush. "I didn't want to talk to the police. They'd twist things around." She swallowed. "But I saw something. I think it matters."

The colors from the nearby bar sign whirred faintly, streaking pink and blue across her pale face. A car passed at the end of the street, tires hissing over the pavement, and Carol flinched, her shoulders jumping. She glanced back again, as if expecting someone to step out of the shadows, her hands worrying the edge of her scarf, twisting it until the fabric bunched tight between her fingers.

"What did you see, exactly?" I asked, keeping my voice low.

Carol's voice trembled. "The week before Liz died, I was closing up the bakery. Around nine-thirty, maybe ten. I was taking the trash out back when I saw someone walking toward her shop while carrying a small wine bottle carrier, like a gift. It had two bottles of wine, I think. And a balloon."

My pulse kicked hard. "A silver balloon?"

She nodded, eyes darting to the street like she expected someone to emerge from the shadows. "A silver balloon. It said *Good Luck* across the front. Like a celebration. I thought maybe it was a store promotion or something. I almost called out, but . . ." She hesitated, her brow pinching. "Then I realized it was Ava Delaney, and I did not want to meddle with her."

My chest went cold. "Are you sure? Are you absolutely positive?"

"As sure as I can be from where I was standing," Carol whispered. "The streetlight hit Ava's hair. That pale blond color, the way she wears it up, you know, you've seen it. She was dressed nice, too, like she'd come from somewhere else. I saw her place the carrier with the two wine bottles and the balloon near the back entrance of Liz's shop. She looked around, like she was making sure no one was watching. She knocked on the door, waited a moment, then left."

I sucked in a gasp. "Did she go inside?"

"No," Carol said quickly. "Just left the package there, after knocking twice. A few minutes later, Liz came out. I guessed she didn't hear the knocking, and she began to lock up, and I saw her pickup the package and carry it inside. I didn't think anything of it until . . ." She swallowed hard. "Until the morning of Liz's death."

The alley seemed to grow darker around us, the light from the street tapering off.

"Carol," I said softly, "you need to tell Detective Hensley what you saw."

Her eyes flicked toward the end of the alley again, pupils wide. "No. I can't. If I tell them, everyone will know it was me. You understand, I'm scared, Claire—people talk in this town. And when they do, it doesn't stop. I've seen what happens when someone sticks their nose where it doesn't belong. I could become the next target!"

She stepped back a pace, her voice lowering to a whisper. "I thought you'd know what to do. You're the one who notices things. You write that world wide web bloggy thing."

I wanted to tell her she'd done the right thing. That she was safe, that she was uninvolved. But even as the words formed, they were empty. It was the kind of reassurance that didn't mean anything when fear was this real.

"Please," Carol whispered, backing away, her scarf fluttering in the cool night breeze. "Don't mention me. Just . . . tell her what I said."

Then she turned and slipped into the shadows, her silhouette swallowed by the dark between the buildings.

I stood there, heart pounding, Carol's words becoming static in my ears.

As I started walking home, the night air bit my skin. Every footstep echoed louder than it should have. I thought about every time I saw Liz at night, enjoying a glass—or three—of wine to end a chaotic day.

If Carol was telling the truth, then the police had been right all along, and Ava wasn't just a suspect anymore.

And whether I liked it or not, that meant something.

I'd keep her name out of it. That much felt non-negotiable. Town had a way of turning whispers into fires, and I wasn't about to toss her into one.

But Detective Hensley still needed to know.

A possible witness. That's what I'd call it. No details that pointed back to Carol. Just enough to make the police look twice.

FORTY

Liz's active case still dominated every whisper, every newspaper, every coffee conversation. The summer murder was all the rage. But now, with Detective Hensley confident in her primary suspect after our in-depth conversation about the witness testimonial and the strength of the case, things were settling.

Justice, or something close to it, was coming.

When Madison suggested a night out, I didn't hesitate. "Let's do it," I said. "Yay, a night of pretending I'm not living inside a true-crime documentary."

Around nine o'clock, we'd taken over three tables on the deck at The Reef Bar. Another beach bar where the drinks were cold, the fries were hot, and the sound of the ocean carried through the open slats of the boardwalk.

Olivia showed up with a neon-yellow clipboard, of all things.

"Okay, logistics," she said, flipping a page. "Guest list, decorations, food, wine, music, and—oh!—dress code. We're not just winging this."

Madison groaned. "Oh my God, Liv. We didn't even sit yet. You're already turning this night into a red-carpet event."

"Excuse me," Olivia said primly, "I prefer the term *elevated rustic aesthetic.*"

Laughter rippled through the group. The feeling of contentment splashed all of us.

Adam showed up halfway through the second round of drinks, his usual easy smile in place. "Hope I'm not crashing the party."

"Not at all," Carly said, scooting over to make room. "We were just talking about the winery."

His grin widened. "Cool! So, I'm exactly where I'm supposed to be."

He pulled up a chair beside me. "My parents are so excited, guys, it's funny to watch. My mom's been on Google and Yahoo searching 'beautiful table arrangements' for days. You're officially getting the Morgan family *treatment.*"

"That sounds like a real thing," I teased.

"Oh, it is," he said. "There will be hundreds of tea lights, cheese boards the size of boogie boards, and a playlist my dad will insist on creating himself. Mostly Fleetwood Mac, if we're lucky."

Everyone tittered, picturing Adam's parents excitedly preparing for their guests.

Olivia was on the new Facebook mobile website through her phone internet browser. "I'm creating the event on Facebook now. Public or private?"

"Private," Madison said quickly. "We don't need half the town showing up just because they heard there's free wine and cheese. We're thinking fifty people max?"

"Done," Olivia said, typing fast. "Okay. Invites going out to our Pilates group, the Driftwood crew, other local shop owners, and anyone in town we love that won't get too messy. Anyone want to add family?"

"Already texted mine," Carly said. "They're in."

I leaned back, sipping my drink, the joy of my friends washing over me.

I wasn't thinking about Liz or Ava or the case. I was thinking about outfits, LimeWire playlists, and appetizers. The things that used to matter before everything went sideways.

Adam caught my eye. "It's going to be a good night, Claire. You deserve it."

I smiled, genuinely. "Yeah. I think it's going to be perfect."

As the night went on, the group thinned out. People were heading home to feed pets or call babysitters. The ocean breeze grew cooler, carrying the scent of clams and beer and late-summer sweetness.

When I finally walked home under the soft glow of the boardwalk lights, my body realized how sleepy my mind was. I would write one blog post before diving headfirst into bed.

*

This Week on the Dunes: Summer Winds Down

Hey friends!

Before the season officially starts to wind down, I just wanted to hop on here and say thank you—truly—for all the kindness, support, and thoughtful messages that have come through lately. The last couple of months have been difficult for our little town. Even with Liz's case still open, the way Coral Haven comes together in hard times never ceases to amaze me.

Support Local While You Can!

As we drift toward fall, a few of our favorite beachside shops will start closing for the season. Make sure to stop by and support them before they take their upcoming, well-deserved winter break!

A few reminders:

- **The Driftwood Café** will keep their summer hours through next weekend. (Pumpkin coffee incoming!)
- **Coral & Tide Boutique** is running their End-of-Season Sidewalk Sale—25% off the whole store!

Grab your favorites now, because once the shutters come down, they won't reopen until spring of next year.

Weekend Forecast: Perfect Beach Days Ahead!

The weather this weekend looks amazing—high 70s, sunny skies, and light coastal breeze. Basically, the kind of weather postcards are jealous of.

And if you're looking for something fun to do, the **annual Coral Haven Surf Competition** kicks off Saturday morning! Even if you don't surf, it's such a good time—music, food trucks, locals cheering like they're at the Olympics. (I'll be there, coffee in hand, pretending I understand wave scores.)

A Note of Gratitude

Over the past few months, I've seen so many of you show up for one another—checking in, sharing information, offering help where you could. Coral Haven has a way of reminding us that even in difficult moments, community really is the heart of everything.

The days are getting shorter now, but the light feels softer, easier somehow.

Here's to a peaceful weekend, some sunshine, and a few more beach weeks before the sweaters come out for good.

Stay kind, stay curious, and don't forget your sunscreen.

—Claire Bear

FORTY-ONE

I hated everything I owned.

Every dress felt wrong. Every pair of pants annoyed me. Even the stuff I used to love suddenly looked like the dumbest purchases of my life.

I stared into my closet for a full thirty seconds, sighed, and said the only reasonable thing.

"Fuck it."

If life was going to keep throwing curveballs, I was at least allowed a small, irresponsible splurge. I grabbed my bag and headed straight for Coral & Tide.

The Coral & Tide Boutique was radiant that afternoon, sunlight streaming through the windows and catching the shimmer of glass jewelry in the display case. The shop sat inside an old Victorian building that had once been a bed-and-breakfast, its white trim faded to cream and its porch wrapped in a chipped teal railing. Inside, the floorboards creaked beneath every step, and a rocky spiral staircase curved up to the second floor where the "fancier" pieces lived.

Clothes filled every inch of space. Finding something you loved felt like a treasure hunt. Prices ranged from *actually affordable* to *definitely for the rich-rich crowd*, but half the fun was guessing which was which before checking the tag.

At the back were two tiny dressing rooms with mismatched curtains hanging from rusty rods that squeaked every time someone pulled them shut. The mirror inside was slightly warped, giving you a taller, thinner version of yourself if you stood at just the right angle. It wasn't perfect, but it gave you the gist.

My birthday was days away, and the winery party had become the talk of every group chat in town. Everyone was buzzing about it. What to wear, what playlist to make, what cheese paired best with rosé.

I couldn't believe how fast the summer was slipping through my fingers. Maybe it was because I'd spent most of it tangled up in a murder investigation I had no business being part of. Interviewing suspects between brunch shifts, chasing leads instead of sunsets and waves. But somehow, here I was, back to something as normal as picking out a birthday dress. The thought felt almost surreal.

But as I flipped through hangers, I seriously could not stop my mind. I kept drifting back to something darker.

The wine bottles. The poison. The balloon.

I couldn't stop thinking about my conversation with Detective Hensley a few days ago, debriefing about the potential witness, and how quickly she'd dismissed the possibility that the Morgan family could be involved. It was true their wines were for sale all over town, but I wondered where Ava had purchased the bottles, if the person who'd sold them to her had come forward. I hadn't asked Detective Hensley, and she hadn't offered.

She'd moved on after that, but the thought had stuck with me; tiny, stubborn, and impossible to shake.

Still, I pushed the doubt aside as I slipped the first dress over my head. It was coral pink and flowy, but too short. The second was white with lace trim. It was pretty, but too "engagement party." The third was the one that made me pause.

A light blue, off-the-shoulder beauty.

A soft, fluttery fabric that swayed like sea foam when I turned in the mirror.

Easy. Effortless. And an added huge bonus, I could eat and drink whatever in it.

I studied my tousled hair, with cheeks slightly sunburned from the walk over. My reflection almost looked like someone who'd made it through the summer unscathed.

And maybe I had.

As I changed back into my clothes, the familiar chatter of the shop surrounded me. Two vacationers debating earrings, someone asking about sale prices. Another patron asking for the sunglass case to be opened.

At the counter, I set the blue dress down, unfolding neatly over my arm. "I think this one's it," I told the acne-riddled teenage cashier.

"Good choice," she said with a grin. "You'll look beautiful. Is it for a special occasion?"

"Yeah. My birthday," I said, smiling back. "This weekend. My friends are throwing a party at the Morgan Family Winery."

"Oh, that sounds like such a pretty place," she said while swiping my card. "My parents say that the lights there at night are gorgeous."

I nodded and smirked. "Yeah. I can't wait."

The card reader beeped, the payment approved, the bag rustled, and that was that. One simple purchase made, one perfect dress for my birthday bash.

I began to reflect on how thankful I was for my friends, who'd stood by me through all the chaos. Thankful for the quiet of daily life returning. Thankful that the only thing on my mind was what shoes to wear with my new dress.

I believed that my part in the whole tragic mess was finally done. I'd helped Detective Hensley as much as I could. The investigation was in good hands now, and soon, justice would be served.

It was time to return to what I loved. I'd keep up my weekly blog posts. Writing about Coral Haven's events, the new businesses popping up, and maybe a few bits of gossip that didn't involve crime scenes. And I'd finally go back to my children's book project, the one that had been sitting half-finished on my desk since all this began. Maybe I'd even find an illustrator, someone who could bring those pages to life the way I saw them in my head.

*

When the notification popped up on my laptop—
*You've been invited to: Claire's 30th Birthday Bash + End of
Season Celebration!*—I laughed out loud. Carly and the girls
had kept the invitation quiet, but seeing my name in that
shiny event header made my chest feel warm. I clicked it
open and instantly smiled at the cover photo: a sun-
drenched vineyard shot from the previous summer, it
looked like, all golden light and laughter.

Reading through the comments made it even better.
People were already tagging each other, planning outfits,
debating who'd bring what dessert. A few inside jokes
from old posts popped up—one about the "Beach Street
Blogger finally turning thirty," another teasing me about
documenting the night "for the archives."

I couldn't help wondering who would show up, and
what they'd bring with them—stories, gifts, secrets, or
something else entirely. I had the jitters, and the happy
excitement you get before a big event, one where you're
the main character.

Facebook Private Event — Hosted by: Carly & the Girls
Event: *Claire's 30th Birthday Bash + End of Season Celebration!*
Location: Morgan Family Winery
Time: Saturday, 4:00 p.m. till the stars come out
Attire: Fun + Cute! Think summer dresses, flowy shirts, and big smiles. There will be *lots* of pictures among the vineyard views.

Details:
Join us for an evening celebrating *Claire Collins* (our favorite blogger + beach babe) and the end of another unforgettable Coral Haven season!
Food and drinks will be provided by the Morgan family—wine tastings, charcuterie, and maybe a few surprises.

Can't wait to see everyone looking fabulous at sunset!

See you soon!

FORTY-TWO

The day before the party, the weather was grossly not cooperating. It was uncomfortably sticky. The late summer humidity made town feel like it might melt into the sea.

I'd just finished cleaning up lunch dishes when my phone started ringing on the counter. Olivia's name flashed across the screen.

"Hey," I answered.

Her voice came through in a breathless rush. "Claire. You need to get downtown right fucking *now*. Something huge is happening."

My heart skipped. "What do you mean, huge?"

"It's Ava," she said. "I'm pretty sure they're arresting her. Right now. Outside The Shore Thing. No shit, everyone and their mother is watching."

For a second, I just stood there, buzzing in my ears, my mind trying to catch up. Once my brain started to comprehend what the hell was going on, I legitimately sprinted to get to Olivia.

By the time I made it to Beach Street, a crowd of onlookers had gathered. The line of parked cars gleamed in the heat, and every storefront window was reflecting the scene like a dozen tiny mirrors. People stood on the sidewalks, eyes wide open, and whispering into their flip phones.

Detective Hensley stood in the center of it all, wearing a crisp navy blazer despite the heat, badge flashing gold in the sun, her posture straight and deliberate. She looked like a boss bitch, calm but dangerous.

Ava stood just outside the shop, her pale hair plastered to her temples, her hands trembling at her sides. Her pink blouse was wrinkled, her mascara smudged beneath her eyes. She looked like someone who'd just woken up from a nightmare and couldn't convince herself it wasn't real.

"I don't understand." Ava's voice cracked, desperate and small. "You've got this wrong! I didn't do anything!" she shrieked.

Hensley didn't flinch. Her tone was steady, almost monotone. "Ava Delaney, you're under arrest for the premeditated murder of Elizabeth Carper."

The words hung in the air like a thunderclap.

Gasps rippled through the growing crowd. Arriving reporters leaned forward, cameras rapidly flashing.

Hensley stepped closer, her voice smooth and practiced as she began reciting the Miranda rights. "You have the right to remain silent. Anything you say can and will be used against you in a court of law . . ."

The rest of her words blurred under the drone of the scattered talking and gasps.

Then there was movement, a figure pushing through the gathering bodies. Bauer.

He stopped a few feet from the tape, frozen. For a second I thought he might shout, defend her, *do* anything, but he just stared. His face was a shifting storm: shock, confusion, guilt, disbelief. His jaw clenched like he was swallowing back a scream.

How does someone even react, I thought, *when the person they love is being arrested for murder?*

He looked traumatized. His whole body rigid, eyes unfocused, like he'd been dropped into some alternate reality. For a flicker of a moment, I almost felt sorry for him. Almost.

Ava's knees buckled slightly as the cuffs clicked shut. "No—no, please," she cried, twisting away. "I didn't kill her! Babe, tell them! Bauer, help! I *swear* I didn't!"

Two uniformed officers caught her by the arms, steady but firm. The metallic clink of the handcuffs echoed off the shop windows like a gunshot. Bauer flinched at the sound, but he didn't move. He didn't defend her. He just stood there, eyes wide, lips parted, the color drained from his face.

From across the street, someone gasped. Another whispered, "Oh my God."

Hensley gave a single nod to her team. "Let's move."

They guided Ava toward the idling patrol car. The sunlight gleamed off the hood, off the cuffs, off the tears streaking her cheeks. She kept shaking her head, sobbing, her voice breaking with every word.

"I was trying to be nice to her!" she choked out. "It was just a gift! You're making a mistake!"

"Yeah, yeah. That's what they all say, princess," an assisting cop chortled out as he guided her head into the open car.

But her voice was swallowed by the sound of the door closing, a hard, final boom that seemed to echo down the street.

The car pulled away slowly, tires crunching over hot pavement, the siren silent but the message unmistakable.

Detective Hensley stood watching for a moment, her face unreadable. She wiped her brow with the back of her hand, gave a few short words to a reporter, and turned away, already decisive, already calculating the next move.

I didn't move. I couldn't. The arrest of Ava was shocking.

Watching the police car disappear down the street, I felt something shift inside me. Not satisfaction, not even relief. Just a deep, hollow exhaustion. Liz was finally getting justice.

Ava was going to be questioned and put away for a long, long time.

And yet, as the patrol lights faded into the sun, a small, unwelcome thought rooted itself in the back of my mind. *Was this really justice?*

Ava looked stunned. The image clung to me: Her wide eyes behind the glass, filled with tears, and her lips trembling like she was about to speak but never got the chance.

Everyone around me seemed so certain. They were already nodding, already whispering about how it made sense, how it all fit. I had a strange feeling in the back of my head that I couldn't shake. Could Ava have done all this by herself? The pieces were all there; they all matched up. But it was almost *too* tidy. Did Bauer really have no idea what Ava had done?

Maybe I was wrong. Maybe this was what justice looked like.

But as the crowd began to thin and the last trace of the police car vanished down Beach Street, an unease lingered in my chest.

Who was I to question it? I wasn't a detective. I wasn't an expert. I was just a blogger with a habit of asking the wrong questions, of digging when I should've stayed quiet.

An amateur writer with a curse for curiosity.

FORTY-THREE

By the time I got home, the AC couldn't keep up with the heat. I kicked off my sandals, poured a glass of water, and turned on the TV, mostly out of habit. I just needed some background noise to fill the silence.

The local news channel flashed onto the screen, and before I could even sit down, there she was.

Ava Delaney.

Her photo filled the top corner of the screen, the same headshot from The Shore Thing's website, next to a red banner that read:

SHOP OWNER ARRESTED IN CORAL HAVEN MURDER INVESTIGATION

The reporter's voice was emotionless; her words made my head dizzy.

"Breaking news this evening out of Coral Haven. Local business owner Ava Delaney, known for the boutique she co-owns with romantic partner Bauer Clips, has been taken into custody in connection with the death of Elizabeth Carper, owner of The Sand Dollar. Investigators are calling the murder *premeditated* and *methodical*, carried out under the guise of a friendly gesture."

B-roll footage appeared. Detective Hensley flashed her badge, officers led Ava toward a police cruiser as onlookers crowded the sidewalk. Bauer in the background, sheet-white and stationary.

"According to police sources, Delaney allegedly delivered two bottles of wine and a balloon reading 'Good Luck' to Carper's shop a week before her death. Toxicology reports confirm the bottles were tampered with and laced with rat poison."

The camera panned to The Sand Dollar's storefront.

"Authorities say Delaney's motive may have been both personal and financial. Her business and romantic ties to Bauer Clips, Carper's former partner, are being closely examined."

Then the anchor's tone shifted slightly, taking on that subtle, practiced gravity that signaled something darker.

"This isn't the first time Delaney's name has surfaced in a suspicious case. Reports confirm she was previously questioned—though never charged—in a separate incident at her former workplace involving the sudden death of a coworker. Sources say toxicology was inconclusive at the time, but investigators are now re-examining that file in light of these new developments."

I was entranced by the television, the words echoing in my head.

"Detective Hensley of the County Police Department confirmed that fingerprints on the poisoned wine bottles, combined with CCTV footage showing Delaney near The Sand Dollar the night before the murder, led to today's arrest. She faces charges of first-degree murder and is currently being held for questioning."

The footage cut to the image of the squad car driving off, Ava's pale face visible through the window, her mouth moving, eyes wild, stricken with tears and still pleading with the officers beside her.

The anchor concluded:

"It's a shocking turn in what many believed was an unsolvable case. Tonight, residents of Coral Haven can rest easier knowing a suspect is finally in custody."

The program switched to commercials, a long-ass new prescription drug ad, a cheerful jingle about coastal vacations, and the healthiest dog food ever.

I sat there, staring at my reflection in the dark glass, my drink sweating on the coffee table. Speechless.

FORTY-FOUR

The late night sullenly settled over us.

The news of Ava's arrest had spread like wildfire in mere minutes. It was all anyone could talk about in texts, the story ping-ponging across every group chat and community page. Headlines. Photos. Speculation.

But in my bungalow that night, things were light and bright. A dark cloud swept away.

Carly arrived around nine with an overnight bag slung over her shoulder and two cans of sparkling lemonade in hand. "Figured we could use a mini slumber party," she said, kicking off her Hollister flip-flops by the door. "To celebrate the fact that we live in a town that's no longer actively being poisoned."

I laughed, the sound coming out easy. "You're not wrong. Come in, my darling."

We made bagel bites, lit a rum-scented candle, and sprawled across my couch while the waves outside rolled their steady rhythm. The day's events began to lift, replaced by that soft, fizzy feeling of relief, the one that comes right before something good.

Carly took a sip of her drink. "So," she said with a teasing grin, "I guess this means Bauer and Ava won't be coming to your party?"

I rolled my eyes. "Even if they were invited—which they weren't—I'm guessing they'll be a little *busy*."

Carly snorted. "Yeah, prison orange isn't really winery chic."

We burst out laughing, not cruelly; a cathartic laugh that came from exhaustion, sleepiness, and disbelief. The sleepy ha-ha's, if you will.

I stood and went to grab the dress I'd picked out that afternoon to show Car. "Okay, but seriously, I want your opinion."

I held it up against me: light blue, off the shoulder, soft and breezy.

Carly gasped. "Oh my God, love love love. That's perfect! It's so *you*. You're gonna look like the human version of a beach day."

"What the hell. What does that even mean?! Is that a good thing? And do you really think so?"

"Absolutely. You just need some statement jewelry."

She hopped up and went straight for my closet, rifling through hangers and drawers until she found a pair of chunky, gold shell earrings and a wide cuff bracelet. "These. You'll sparkle under the string lights at the winery."

I laughed as she tossed them on the bed. "You're like a personal stylist and a hype woman all in one."

"Obviously," she said, mock-bowing. "It's in the friendship contract."

We spent the next hour finalizing the last of the party details. Going over who was bringing what, how to handle the iTunes playlist, and whether to assign a designated photographer with Carly's digital camera. The Facebook event had already hit nearly forty-five confirmed guests, including most of our friends who are shop owners, some of the Pilates crew, parents that I babysat for, and a few of the girls' old high school friends that I'd befriended in the last couple years.

"Tomorrow's going to be amazing," Carly said, tucking her legs beneath her on the couch. "Great weather, good people, wine. What more could we want?"

I nodded, smiling. "Yeah. I think it'll be the perfect way to end the season."

For a while, we just listened to the ocean through the cracked window. The sound of the waves created a perfect nighttime ambiance.

The case was solved. The town could rest. We could celebrate.

And as I blew out the candle before heading to bed, I let myself believe it too.

*

The morning of my birthday felt impossibly pleasant. The daytime looked like it was pictured by an artist. I woke up to sunlight spilling across my sheets, soft and golden. For once, I didn't have anywhere urgent to be. Just my birthday, and the quiet promise of a day that might go right without ridiculous rumors.

Carly practically kicked my door down promptly at eight. "Happy birthday, player. Yoga? Pilates? Let's be our best selves before we ruin it later."

I loudly groaned, then sneakily chuckled and threw on a pair of black flared yoga pants. We walked together to the studio, yammering on about the upcoming evening. The air was already warm with that morning summer breeze. Inside, the room smelled faintly of eucalyptus and cleaned rubber mats. The instructor's voice was soothing, all talk of grounding and gratitude, but I mostly forced myself not to fall asleep during shavasana.

Afterward, we grabbed smoothies from the little beach shack down the street before heading our separate ways. Carly had errands for the party prep; I had my own kind of ritual to keep.

*

First stop was Daisy's Nails. I'd been going to Daisy since I moved here; she knew my polish preferences better than I did.

"Birthday girl!" she said when I walked in, grinning from behind the counter. "You ready for your usual?"

"Of course," I said, sliding into the chair. "Acrylics, pale pink. Maybe a little shimmer."

While she worked, the salon was busy with chatter. The nail drills whirring, dryers banging, and women in pedicure chairs flipping through magazines they never actually read.

And, of course, gossip.

I should've known it would come up the second I sat down. Daisy lowered her voice just enough to make it more dramatic. "So," she said, leaning closer, "can you believe about Ava Delaney? They actually arrested her. Right there outside the shop!"

The woman two seats over perked up instantly. "I saw the photos online! You could practically see her makeup streaks. And Bauer? Poor guy looked like he'd seen a ghost."

Daisy snorted, shaking her head as she filed my nails. "Poor guy? Please. He just stood there, frozen like an idiot. Didn't even say a word. If my lover watched me get arrested, I'd expect at least *something*. Some sort of support."

I laughed under my breath. "I think the whole town's still trying to process it."

"Oh, honey, they're not processing. They're *thriving*." She grinned, glancing toward the other nail techs. "We've talked about nothing else. It's better than cable."

The elderly woman across from us chimed in. "You just never really know people, huh? She always seemed so put together these last few months."

Daisy nodded. "And now she's in handcuffs. Wild." She finished the last stroke of polish, blowing gently on my fingertips. "You're lucky, Claire. You're normal. Well, normal-ish. I don't trust anyone who color-codes their closet."

I smiled faintly, unsure whether to laugh or agree. "Yeah. Totally normal," I said, thinking about every quirk I had.

She tilted her head. "Eyebrows too?"

"You know me too well," I said.

Twenty minutes later, I left with perfect acrylic tips, freshly shaped brows, and the faint high that only acetone fumes and small-town scandal could give you.

*

Afternoon rolled around, and the temperature hovered at a comfortable seventy-eight degrees. A light sea gust carried the faint scent of salt and honeysuckle through the air as I waited on my porch steps, holding my little woven clutch and watching for Olivia's car.

When her dirty white Camry finally pulled up, music was already thumping from the open windows. Madison leaned out from the back seat and yelled, "Get in loser, we're going shopping. Just kidding, HAPPY BIRTHDAY!"

I full-belly laughed, locking my door behind me and sliding into the front passenger seat. Carly waved from the back, polarized honey-green sunglasses perched on her nose and a tote bag full of food beside her.

"Okay," Olivia said, pulling away from the curb. "Sun's out, playlist's queued, and the vibes are immaculate."

*

The drive to the Morgan Family Winery was short.

The road curved gently through back brush of emerald green, the sun catching on every leaf and tendril. Rows upon rows of grapevines stretched across many acres, their clusters ripening beneath the late-summer light. The land smelled of earth and fruit and distant ocean air.

The Morgan estate sat gracefully atop the only hill near Coral Haven. An old farmhouse-turned-winery surrounded by manicured gardens, with lanterns strung between weathered beams. A line of Edison bulbs zigzagged across the open courtyard, already glowing faintly in the afternoon light, ready to turn golden once dusk arrived.

Hanging lights wove through the trees, creating a romantic canopy over sleek, cream outdoor furniture and polished wooden tables draped with crisp linen cloths. A low firepit sat at the center of a stone patio, piled high with kindling, waiting to be lit once the sun went down.

"Wow," Madison whispered, pressing a hand to the window. "They outdid themselves. This looks incredible."

The *Happy 30th Birthday, Claire!* banner fluttered in the breeze, tastefully strung across the entryway in white and gold. Balloons bobbed near the steps, their gold ribbons glinting.

We parked near the vineyard's edge, gravel crunching under the tires. The faint whisper of laughs and clinking glasses drifted from the barn at the center of the property.

The barn itself was breathtaking. It was a wide, open structure with whitewashed walls and tall sliding doors flung open to reveal tables lined with charcuterie boards, platters of fruit, and bottles of wine neatly arranged beneath hanging ivy. The far wall was dominated by a sturdy bar of reclaimed wood.

As I stepped out of the car, the hem of my light blue dress brushed against my legs. The breeze caught the fabric, and I felt electric. Excited. Alive. Pretty.

What Happened to Liz

And yet, underneath the excitement, a small tingle of something colder stirred.

Maybe it was nerves. Maybe it was just the surreal calm after everything that had happened.

Carly linked arms with me, dragging me forward. "Come on, birthday girl. Let's get some wine in you. Actually, on second thought, let's get a *lot* of wine in you."

As we walked up the path, I spotted George and Jenna Morgan standing near the barn entrance, radiant in their summer attire. Adam was beside them, wide mouth grinning as he waved us over.

"There she is!" Jenna called, her voice bright and warm. "The woman of the hour!"

I smiled as she handed me a glass of deep red wine, the sun glistening off the glass.

"You look *stunning*, dear," she said, admiring my dress. "That blue color suits you perfectly."

"Thank you," I said, returning her smile. "This place looks amazing. You all really outdid yourselves."

"Oh, it's our pleasure," George said, straightening the edge of a tablecloth. "We're just happy to have the winery filled with friends and laughter again. It's been a depressing couple of months."

I nodded, taking a small sip of the wine, a cabernet sauvignon, rich and full, with a velvety bite that lingered on my tongue.

Adam smiled, holding up his own glass. "To the past staying in the past and new beginnings, right?"

"Right," I said softly.

The string lights above us swayed in the breeze, their spark slowly brightening as the sun dipped lower in the sky. Laughter and music floated from the barn. Someone uncorked another bottle, and the day filled with the scent of oak and grapes and summer happiness.

I was delighted.

FORTY-FIVE

The sun slipped behind the tree line, and the winery had transformed into something out of a dream.

Music pulsed through the open barn—Beyoncé, Justin Timberlake, Rihanna—all the classics downloaded from iTunes years ago and living their second life through a Bluetooth speaker that somehow hadn't died yet.

Laughter spread across the courtyard like spilled champagne. Someone started an unsuccessful conga line near the bar. Someone else tripped and nearly broke the Ping-Pong table.

I couldn't stop smiling.

"Claire!" someone called. I turned to see Megan, one of the moms I babysat for, waving from across the lawn. "Happy birthday, sweetheart! You look gorgeous! Wow, nice dress, is that from Coral and Tide?"

"Thank you! Yes!" I said, giving her a quick hug. Megan's husband was holding their toddler, who had a juice box in one hand and was trying to grab a balloon with the other. "You made it!"

"Wouldn't miss it," she said. "You've earned some fun after the season we've all had."

Next came Tanya and Liam from the Pilates studio, toasting me with glasses of rosé. "This is incredible," Tanya said, eyes scanning the vineyard. "How do we convince the Morgans to host every party from now on?"

"Bribery," I said, laughing. "Lots of bribery . . . and get Carly to help you."

Inside the barn, Derek and Emily from The Driftwood waved from behind a platter of cheese cubes. Emily shouted over the music, "We brought the brie! Don't say I never contribute!"

I made my rounds, thanking everyone for coming, hugging friends I hadn't seen in weeks, and trying to soak in every shimmer of light, every burst of laughter, every song beat vibrating through the floorboards.

At one point, Rihanna's "Pon de Replay" came on, and Madison and Olivia dragged me to the dance floor. We screamed the lyrics, arms up, hair sticking to our faces, the sweet taste of wine lathering our taste buds.

The bonfire crackled to life outside, casting warm light over the group. Guests lingered on picnic blankets and chairs, sipping slowly, the night soft and alive.

That's when Adam appeared at my elbow, two glasses of cabernet in hand.

"Birthday girl needs a refill," he said with that easy grin, handing me one.

"Adam! You've outdone yourself. This place looks incredible."

He shrugged modestly. "It's my parents, mostly. They love a reason to celebrate." He paused, swirling his drink, eyes flicking briefly toward the vineyard where the string lights dipped into the distance. "I just . . . wish things were different. I've been worried about Bauer. The whole Ava thing's really—"

Before he could finish, Madison popped up beside us, nearly spilling her drink. "Nope!" she said firmly. "Not tonight, mister. No murder talk at the birthday party. We're done with all that drama. Tonight's about *Claire*."

Adam blinked, then chuckled softly. "Fair enough. Can't argue with that."

He clinked his glass lightly against mine. "To you, Claire. The calm in the chaos."

The words made me smile, even though something about the way he said them brushed cold against my spine.

I shook it off, laughing as Madison tugged me back to the dance floor.

The music shifted to Justin Timberlake's "Cry Me A River," and soon the whole barn was melodically singing along. People were dancing on the lawn, shoes abandoned, arms around each other.

Candles flickered on tabletops. Someone passed around chocolate cupcakes. The firepit blazed higher, sparks floating up into the darkening sky like tiny stars.

*

The night had settled into its perfect rhythm, my cheeks hurt from smiling. Olivia and Mads were already halfway through our ridiculous, half-sober "Single Ladies" routine, and the crowd was eating it up like we were headlining a music festival.

When the song ended, I grabbed my drink and sank into a chair, breathless, my skin warm from dancing. That's when I saw Carly making a beeline toward me.

The bar lights glowed soft and honey-colored, the shouting around us loosening into comfortable chaos.

Carly dropped into the empty seat beside me. Her perfume hit first, sharp and sweet, followed by a smile that didn't quite reach her eyes. Under the lights, her gaze looked glassy.

"Happy birthday, Claire," she said, her words slightly slurred but still steady enough to carry a sting. "You having fun?"

"Yeah," I said, smiling because it was easier than thinking. "It's been a weird month, but—"

"Weird," she repeated, leaning in closer. "You know what's weird? Finding out your best friend's been asking around about old drama and suspects—like she's trying to solve a murder by throwing her best friend under the bus."

My stomach twisted. "Carly."

"No, really," she snapped, lifting her glass and sloshing a bit onto the table. "Why, Claire? Why meddle in something that had nothing to do with you? Did you really think I had anything to do with Liz's death? Or was that just good blog material?"

Her voice sliced through the noise, sharp enough that a few people turned their heads.

Heat rushed to my face. "No—God, Carly, I never said that. I never thought that. I just—"

She gave a small, humorless laugh. "You just what? Stirred the pot? You think everyone's a character in your story, don't you? Bauer, Liz, me." Her voice faltered for half a second before she added, softer, "You don't know half of what went on between us. You never did."

The words hit harder than I wanted them to. Maybe it was the alcohol, or the guilt that had been simmering for weeks, but something inside me cracked.

"I'm sorry," I said too fast, my voice too shaky. "I didn't mean to make things worse. I thought—" I swallowed, forcing the words out. "I thought I was helping. I swear, I never meant to hurt you."

Carly stared at me for a moment, her lips parting as if she might say something else. Then she just laughed again, a quiet, bitter sound. "Helping," she echoed, shaking her head. "You really don't know when to stop, do you?"

Her tone wasn't cruel. It was weary. And somehow, that hurt worse.

I opened my mouth to reply, but nothing came. The room suddenly felt too bright, too hot. My pulse pounded in my ears.

"I—uh—I'll be right back," I managed, pushing my chair back. The floor swayed a little beneath me, that tipsy edge between dizzy and clear. "Just need a minute. I'm so sorry." I sprinted away.

*

I was a little too drunk to brush off the urge. The very real, very urgent need to pee.

I begrudgingly groaned because of the drunken conversation with Carly, and I began glancing around while doing a little "don't pee right now" dance. The two bathrooms at the back of the barn had been occupied all night, a constant line of girlfriends chatting, wine glasses in hand. I walked over, hoping maybe I'd catch a break.

Occupied. Both.

I did another small desperate little bounce in place. "Seriously?"

As I turned back toward the tables, I spotted Jenna Morgan near the dessert spread, chatting with George and one of the Pilates girls.

"Hey, Jenna!" I called, trying not to sound as urgent as I felt. "Are there any other bathrooms around? Both of these are full, and I—"

Jenna smiled kindly, brushing a stray curl from her face. "Oh, honey, yes! There's one inside the house. Just go right up the walkway and through the side door—you can't miss it. It's much quicker. Be fast!"

"Thank you!"

"Of course! Don't tell anyone I sent you, or they'll all start sneaking in there!" she teased.

I laughed and waved before heading toward the main house. Already forgetting the heated conversation with Carly.

The residential farmhouse loomed just beyond the edge of the vineyard. Two stories painted white with wide black shutters and a deep wraparound porch. Light shone from a few of the downstairs bulbs, golden and warm.

As I walked up the gravel path, the music from the party grew fainter until it was just a distant beat of Beyoncé's voice carrying on the breeze.

The house smelled faintly of oak and wine, the air cooler inside than I expected. I slipped off my shoes at the door out of habit, feeling oddly like an intruder even though I'd been invited.

"Bathroom," I whispered to myself, scanning the hall. Where would the bathroom be?

It didn't take long to find it. It was a neat little half bath tucked upstairs in the hallway. I exhaled in relief, flipped on the light, and let myself finally relax.

FORTY-SIX

When I stepped out, something caught my attention.

A narrow hallway led deeper into the house, lined with framed photos. Family portraits, vineyard awards, and a few shots of Adam in his teens at harvest festivals. One photo showed Adam and Bauer together, arms slung around each other, smiling wide and sunburned, holding up a Little League trophy.

I paused, tilting my head.

I'd heard they were close once. Coral Haven wasn't a big place, and people's lives overlapped easily. Still, something about the photo struck me. Bauer's expression was open, easy. Adam's was different. Admiration. Almost reverence.

I moved farther down the hall. Curiosity bloomed against my better judgment.

A door was slightly ajar near the end.

I hesitated, glancing back down toward the front door. The music outside was still muffled and distant. I could hear banter, maybe Olivia's voice.

I looked out the hallway window where the sound was coming from and saw Olivia, half-hidden behind the side of the house. It took me a second to register what I was seeing. She was pressed up against the cook, Sean, his hands braced on either side of her hips, both tangled in a kiss that was definitely *not* rated for public viewing.

I froze, then smiled. Olivia, the shyest one of us, who used to blush if a guy so much as winked at her, now hooking up with Sean like she'd been waiting her whole life to do it.

She was way out of his league. Sean with his perpetual scruff, salt-stained sneakers, and greasy hair—but watching them, I couldn't help but feel happy for her. It was so nice to see that one of us was getting some.

The moment was too hot to interrupt, so I turned away quickly, giving them their privacy.

I started jamming with the faint music and in my drunken stupor, I remembered I was exploring.

I reached the slightly open door. *Just a peek*, I told myself. *You're curious, that's all.*

The door creaked softly as I pushed it open.

The room was instantly recognizable. Adam's.

It smelled like cedar and something sharper, almost metallic. The bed was neatly made, the corners tucked tight. A boring black comforter and one pillow on his bed. Books and old vinyl records lined the shelves. A desk sat by the window, with thoroughly arranged and organized colored pens, papers squared off, nothing out of place.

But what drew my eye was the wall above the desk, faint outlines of where pictures had been recently taken down. The wallpaper was slightly lighter in squares and rectangles.

Weird.

A small, closed laptop sat on the desk, and beside it, a thick folder with *Bauer Clips* written in fading ink. I ran my finger over it. A dozen questions swirled in my mind.

Why would Adam have that?

My pulse hastened. I stepped back, scanning the room again.

A dresser. A nightstand. A closet.

The walk-in closet door was closed tight.

Something about the way it stood there, shut but inviting; it tugged at me.

I swallowed hard, forcing a nervous laugh. "You're being ridiculous," I whispered to myself. "You're snooping because you've had too much wine. Do it and run back to the party."

But then another sound drifted faintly through the wall, the muffled thrum of the party, the girls shouting for me to come back for the dance.

I took a slow breath, staring at that closet door. *Just one look. Then you'll go back. You'll dance. You'll laugh. You'll forget all of this.*

My hand hovered over the doorknob.

And then I turned it.

*

The knob turned easily beneath my hand, and for a breathless moment, I paused.

Then I opened the door.

A faint, stale chill rolled out, brushing against my legs. The smell hit first—paper, glue, and something masked underneath, like metal or disinfectant.

At first, I couldn't process what I was looking at. My brain rejected it, scrambled for a logical shape.

It wasn't clothes hanging in that large closet.

It was . . . Bauer?

His face stared back at me from every wall. Hundreds of photographs, taped and tacked, layered on top of each other like a madman's collage. Some glossy and new, some brittle and yellowed with age. His smile repeated again and again, until it didn't feel like a smile at all. Just an image devouring itself.

Some of the photos were slashed with red marks, the ink bled into the paper, dried into jagged streaks. Others were meticulously cut, leaving white-edged holes where faces used to be.

I stepped closer, my heartbeat echoing in my ears.

A row of pictures showed Bauer and Liz at summer markets, the boardwalk, and the shop. Her face neatly snipped out of each one. Another series captured Bauer with Ava walking outside. Across each photo, a black "X" carved through her features, pen scribbles repeatedly tearing through the paper.

And in the very center, one large photo of Bauer holding a bottle of wine, smiling toward the camera, had thick red Sharpie scrawled across it in furious, looping letters:

HE LOVES ME.

The words bled through the paper, seeping onto the photo beneath it.

My throat went dry. The room tilted slightly, the air pressing close around me.

Below the collage, a low shelf had been turned into some kind of shrine. I crouched to look, drawn by horrified curiosity.

There were small objects arranged with unsettling precision: a guitar pick glinting under the bulb, a silver key, a faded blue T-shirt folded perfectly in half. The tag had been torn out, but I recognized the name faintly printed near the hem. *Bauer Clips*.

His old high school football uniform hung in a shadow box, perfectly centered, the glass polished to an immaculate shine. A faded game program was pinned beside it, the pages curling with age.

Next to the shirt, a small, wide Ziploc bag—empty—lay half-hidden under a folded napkin. I lifted it with shaking fingers. The inside was dusted faintly white.

There were newspaper clippings too. Dozens of them. Bauer's name circled again and again in red. Indents in the paper. Headlines like:

LOCAL ATHLETE WINS REGIONAL CHAMPIONSHIP
YOUNG MAN SAVES CAT IN TREEE
COMMUNITY RALLIES AROUND CORAL HAVEN FAVORITE

Every word of praise was underlined, starred, worshipped.

And then there was the jewelry box.

It sat open on the small shelf, lined in dark blue velvet, filled with something that looked disturbingly personal. A shiver ran through my spine when I realized what the contents were. Human hair. Blond. Bauer's hair.

I stepped back, brushing my shoulder with something metal and cold.

A foldable worktable latched against the wall slammed down, and I jumped. Its surface was littered with pages. Sketches of wine bottles, dosage notes written in small block handwriting, mathematical formulas scrawled down the sides.

Next to the haphazardly hung papers sat a cardboard box with its lid half off. Inside, a nearly empty container of rat poison rested beside a few used syringes. The faint chemical tang of it stung my nose.

For a moment, I couldn't move.

Every object around me blurred together. The photos, the ink, the scent of metal and dust and something faintly sweet, like decaying fruit.

My body knew before my mind could name it.

The realization hit like a physical blow.

Adam.

Adam had done this. Adam murdered Liz.

He'd poisoned Liz.

He'd framed Ava.

He'd built an entire world around Bauer. Obsessing over him, loving him, wanting to *be* him.

A chill rippled through me, every hair standing on end.

I backed away, my hand pressed over my mouth to stop the sound clawing up my throat.

And then, faintly, and beyond the distant bass of the party outside, I heard it—the sound of footsteps pounding up the stairs.

Weighty. Rapid.

Coming closer.

FORTY-SEVEN

The footsteps grew louder.

Pounding up the stairs.

My whole body locked up, my pulse roaring in my ears. My ears perked up, and my fingers were still gripping the edge of a cardboard box. I turned just as Adam appeared in the doorway, his outline framed by the hall light.

He stopped short. For half a second, he looked surprised and then confused, almost as if he'd walked into the wrong room. Then his eyes darted past me, landing on the open closet.

Everything about him shifted. His posture toughened, his expression tensed, and I watched the exact moment he realized what I'd seen.

"You shouldn't be in here," he said, monotonal.

My mouth went dry. "Adam . . . what is this?"

He didn't answer right away. His gaze flicked from me to the closet again, scanning the wall of photos and notes in sight, the shrine I'd uncovered. I could practically see his mind racing. How much had I seen, how long had I been standing there?

"So," he finally said, voice low, almost calm, "you found it. It would be you who found it, fucking snoop," he muttered.

"I—" I swallowed hard. "Why do you have all this stuff about Bauer? About Liz? About Ava?"

A short, snipped laugh escaped him. "You weren't supposed to see this. Nobody was."

He took a step toward me. I took one back.

"Adam," I said quietly, "just listen. We can go downstairs. Forget this happened."

He smiled, but there was nothing warm in it. "You think it's that simple?"

I forced a shaky nod. "Yes. It can be. I won't tell anyone."

He shook his head slowly. "You can't unsee it, Claire. You can't unlearn what you just found. You talk to Hensley. You write about everything that happens in this godforsaken town. You think I don't know that? You'd ruin everything. So much time, so much planning."

His voice trembled, not with fear, but anger.

"You framed Ava. Why?" I whispered.

"You figured it out. I *freed* Bauer," he said. "Liz was a parasite. She used him. When they broke up, I thought it was finally over, but then Ava showed up. And she was worse. Always so smug. Always in the way."

I stared at him, stunned. "So you poisoned Liz? Why?"

"She left me no choice," he said, like he honestly believed it. "She didn't deserve him, and she was bad for business. A nuisance really. I've loved Bauer since we were kids. You don't understand what that's like—to see someone so good, so perfect, and know you could be the one who makes his life better."

My body flushed and I turned toward him. "Adam . . . you're scaring me."

He stepped closer. "Do you know what it's like to watch him with other people? To see him waste his time on women who don't care about or love him the way I do?"

He was pacing now, agitated, voice breaking in and out. "It started small. Just keeping track of things he liked. His food, his music, his shirts. I just wanted to understand him. To *be* like him. And then . . . it became something else. Something much more."

I could see the sweat beading on his temple, the way his fingers twitched.

"When Liz came along," he continued, "I tried to ignore it. I really did. But she didn't appreciate him. And when he left her, I was *so happy*. Finally, it would be me. But then Ava came. And Bauer . . . He just replaced her. He always replaces them."

"Adam—"

"I had to fix it!" he shouted, the words echoing off the walls. "I had to take back control. Liz was the problem. She had to go. And framing Ava . . . It was perfect. Everything lined up."

My heart was racing so fast it hurt. "You're not making any sense. This isn't love, Adam. This is obsession. Adam, this isn't right."

He blinked at me, almost pitying. "You don't get to define it. I know what love is. I've lived it every single fucking day since middle school."

I backed away until his computer desk poked my hip. "You need help. I can get you help."

He smiled faintly, and that's when I realized he was done talking. He'd said too much, and he knew it.

"You shouldn't have come in here," he said softly, almost sadly. "You should've just danced."

The sound of laughter from the party floated faintly through the window, so bright and unreal compared to the cold silence between us.

And in that silence, I knew: whatever mask Adam had been wearing all these years had just fallen away.

*

The second Adam lunged forward, I reached for the closest object, the bedside lamp. My fingers brushed the cool brass base. One good swing, that's all I needed. But he was faster.

His hand clamped around my wrist, twisting just enough to make the lamp slip from my grasp. It hit the floor with a thunderous crack, the bulb popping and the room plunging into half-shadow.

"Don't," he hissed.

I stumbled back, my heart hammering. "Adam, stop—please."

He took a step forward, voice trembling with fury. "You shouldn't have come up here. You shouldn't have seen my things, you bitch."

Then all hell broke loose.

His shoulder slammed into mine, driving me backward. My elbow struck the nightstand and immediate pain lit up my arm. The lamp cord whipped across my face as I tried to duck away, shoving at his chest. I tasted metal and something dripped onto my chin. We crashed into the nightstand again. Cologne bottles rolled like marbles across the hardwood. The air filled with the sharp tang of bergamot and the unpleasant scent of burnt, broken glass.

"Someone will hear us! HELP, HELP!" I gasped, screamed, my voice raw.

"No one's fucking coming, Claire," he snapped, reaching for me again.

The scene was chaos. Shards crunching underfoot, piercing skin. I twisted, kicked, anything to make space. The alarm clock hit the floor, blaring an erratic beep until it went silent under his heel.

He tried to pin my arms above my head. His breath ragged against my ear. "Just stop fighting," he muttered through his teeth. "It'll be easier if you stop."

I shoved with every ounce of strength left in me. We slammed into the closet; photos fluttered down like startled birds, newspaper clippings flying messily around the room, ruining the shrine—Bauer's face everywhere, torn, taped, slashed, staring.

"Look what you've done!" Adam shouted, voice cracking, angry tears forming at the corner of his eyes.

I scrambled, catching the edge of the dresser to steady myself. "Adam, listen to me! Please, I won't tell . . ."

But he wasn't listening. His eyes were wild, glassy, unseeing. The calm, smiling Adam from beach days and barbecues was gone. What stood in front of me was frantic, obsessive, and broken.

"You ruined everything. She ruined everything," he whispered.

The party outside kept going, music muffled, so close, and yet another world away.

I drew in a shaky breath, ready to make one last push toward the door.

Then his shadow rose over me. His hands closed around my throat in a single, practiced motion.

At first it was pressure, then heat, then the terrifying realization that no air was coming. The room shrank to a tunnel of fractured light. My pulse roared in my ears, slow, uneven.

I clawed at his wrists, scratching deep enough to draw blood. My heels slipped on the spilled cologne. My vision pulsed white at the edges. The world tilted, the ceiling spinning overhead.

A thought flickered in my brain of Liz, of how it must have felt as the poison took hold. How the veil of death must've slipped over her slowly, quietly, until there was nothing left to fight with.

The light fractured again. The sounds faded, draining away like water.

Then.

A crash. A shout. More footsteps thundering up the stairs.

Somewhere beyond the ringing in my head, a door burst open. Voices, jagged and distant, cut through the blur.

"What the fuck is going on up here?"

The words echoed, folding into a low hum as everything went black.

FORTY-EIGHT

I woke to noise. Not sound, but chaos. Voices colliding. Footsteps pounding. Someone shouting my name, or maybe just shouting.

For a split second, I had no idea where I was. Then the memory crashed back into me all at once. Adam's room.

I must've been out for seconds, maybe less, but everything was spinning. My eyes snapped open, and the world tilted violently, the floor and ceiling trading places. The noise around me felt close, suffocating, but my brain lagged, refusing to process it all at once.

The ceiling fan spun lazily above, its blades stuttering in and out of focus like a broken film reel. My pulse beating in my ears. I tried to move and sit up, but pain exploded through my neck and shoulders, radiating down my spine until I gasped.

"Easy, Claire," a familiar voice said, low and firm.

Detective Hensley knelt beside me, one hand on my arm, her eyes scanning my face. Behind her, madness filled the room. Around me, uniformed officers were crowding in, radios squawking, the sound of someone thrashing against restraints.

Adam.

He was on the floor near the door, hands cuffed behind his back, his face red and wild as he struggled against the officer holding him down. "You don't understand!" he yelled. "She ruined everything! That bitch ruined everything! She—"

"Get him out of here," Hensley snapped, but remained poised. Her voice cut through the noise like a blade.

Two officers hauled Adam to his feet. He twisted, his eyes locking on me. For a second, there was something in them, rage, desperation, something I didn't want to name. Then he was gone, pulled out of the room and down the stairs.

The moment he disappeared, my body started shaking. The adrenaline finally caught up, washing through me like a wave I couldn't stop.

"Hey, hey." Hensley's hand pressed gently on my shoulder. "You're safe now, Claire. You did such a great job. You're okay."

"I—" My throat was on fire, my voice barely there. "How did you know? How did you—"

She gave a small, knowing smile, though her eyes were tired. "Let's chalk it up to right place, right time. We have a lot of catching up to do. The last twenty-four hours have been . . . something."

I blinked at her, the edges of her words not quite sinking in. I repeated, "You—how did you know to come here?"

Her radio crackled, interrupting. "Unit Twelve, suspect in custody. Victim conscious. Requesting medical on scene."

A wave of static followed, and a voice on the other end replied with a string of numbers I didn't recognize. Hensley pressed the receiver to her mouth. "Copy that. Send them in."

I could hear footsteps pounding up the stairs again. This time there were more officers, paramedics, urgent, organized chaos.

Hensley stayed crouched beside me. "You're going to be checked out by the medics, okay? They'll take you to the hospital for evaluation. Just to be safe."

I nodded weakly, though I could barely feel my head move. My pulse still thudded against my temples. The air in the room was full with dust and the faint scent of spilled cologne and sweat. I briefly look down and noticed a red, wet substance all over my legs and arms. Blood.

Downstairs, the music had stopped. Through the open window, I could hear voices from the party, confused, frightened conversations drifting up from the courtyard.

As Hensley helped me to my feet, pain shot up my leg, sharp and blinding. I sucked in a breath; my bare foot looked like a red-and-white Jackson Pollock painting, glass still biting into my skin. Blood smeared beneath me, dark and slick.

She tightened her grip instinctively, steadying me as she guided me toward the hallway. Her radio crackled to life again, a jumble of police codes I couldn't translate. She gave the slightest nod to the officer entering the room, then turned back to me, her eyes dropping briefly to my foot before lifting to meet mine.

"Come on," she said softly. "Let's get you out of here."

The staircase seemed impossibly long. Each step creaked beneath us, the sound of chatter and disbelief growing louder with every step.

When we reached the bottom, the scene hit me like a wave.

Dozens of faces. Friends, coworkers, neighbors, people who'd spent their summers drinking wine under fairy lights stood frozen in disbelief. Some whispered. Some cried. Others just stared as the officers led Adam, handcuffed and hollow-eyed, through the center of it all.

The flashing patrol lights outside spilled through the windows, painting everyone in harsh sweeps of red and blue.

"Is that Adam?" someone gasped.

"What's going on?"

"I thought Ava—"

"She's innocent, then?"

"Why, Adam? How?"

The questions spread like fire through dry brush, one sparking the next.

Then I saw Adam's parents pushing through the crowd. Their faces were ashen, disbelief written across every line. George's voice cracked as he shouted, "Adam! What is this? What did you do?"

Jenna's hands trembled as she reached toward him, her pearl bracelet jingling with every movement. "We were about to sing 'Happy Birthday,' and now—now this? What did you do, Adam . . ." Her voice broke, raw and disbelieving. "What did we do wrong?"

Adam didn't answer. His eyes were distant, as if he'd already left the room in every way that mattered.

Detective Hensley stepped between them, calm but firm. "Please step back, Mr. and Mrs. Morgan. We'll answer your questions at the station."

George's face crumpled, confusion giving way to grief. "He wouldn't hurt anyone," he muttered, voice cracking. "He's my son. He wouldn't . . ."

But the cuffs gleamed under the flashing lights, and the truth hung in the air.

Hensley's hand stayed steady on my back as she guided me toward the door. The cool night air hit like a slap, cutting through the heat and the noise. Outside, an ambulance waited, headlights piercing the dark.

I stood barefoot on the porch steps, my body numb, my mind going in and out of awareness. The crowd blurred into color and sound. Sirens, shouting, crying.

And then dizziness.

Just the spinning cop lights fading as my knees gave way, and the world went dark. Again.

FORTY-NINE

My eyes opened and it was like surfacing from underwater. My eyelids fluttered, and for a second, I thought I was still in that room.

My vision sharpened just enough for me to realize I was strapped to a stretcher in the back of an ambulance, parked out front of the Morgan house.

Pain split through my head, sharp and brutal, like my skull was coming apart from the inside. A metallic taste coated my tongue, thick and sour, making my stomach churn.

"Easy, easy. She's awake," a paramedic said.

A hand pressed gently against my shoulder to keep me still. The ambulance smelled like bleach and exhaust, and every sound was too close. Radios, voices, the crackle of static.

Through the open ambulance doors, I could see the front of Adam's house glowing with lights. The party that had been laughter and music an hour ago was now a blur of horrified faces and flashing police vehicles.

Adam was being led down the front lawn by two male officers, wrists cuffed tight behind his back. His face was pale and streaked with sweat. He stumbled once, and Detective Hensley caught his arm, pushing him forward.

"Adam Morgan," she said, her voice hard. "You're under arrest for the premeditated murder of Liz Carper."

He twisted against the cuffs, his voice cracking with panic. "You don't understand! Bauer needs me! He *needs* me! I can't go to jail—who's going to take care of him?"

Hensley's expression didn't change. "Keep moving."

"Bauer doesn't even know what's good for him!" Adam shouted, his voice rising above the murmuring crowd. "She ruined everything! I fixed it—I *fixed it!*"

The officers shoved him toward the police SUV, its lights cutting red across his face.

He turned once, just before they slammed the door, and for a split second his eyes met mine through the blur of lights. There was no remorse in them, just confusion. As if he still couldn't understand why I'd ruined his perfect plan.

My ears were ringing again, voices overlapping. Detective Hensley barking instructions, radios spitting codes, people whispering my name.

"She's okay, she's breathing," someone said.

"Pulse is steady."

"Let's keep her talking."

But I couldn't concentrate. Everything blurred together once more.

Then I heard crying. Familiar crying.

I turned my head, and through the open door I saw them, my friends. Madison, Olivia, Carly. All huddled together near the porch. Their makeup streaked, faces blotchy from tears.

"Oh my God, Claire," Madison whimpered, covering her mouth with trembling fingers. Olivia next to her, too distraught to speak. Her eyes were wide, already glossy with tears. "We told you this wasn't a game. You could've died!"

Madison stood beside the ambulance door, her voice climbing an octave as she shifted into nurse mode. "I'm not letting you lift a finger for the next week. Seriously. You're officially under medical surveillance—my medical surveillance. I'll check on you every hour, and my phone will be on twenty-four-seven for any medical inquiries."

Even through the ache in my neck, I managed a small laugh. "Madison, you're ridiculous."

"I'm serious," she pressed, rummaging through her oversized purse like she might pull out a defibrillator at any second. "I have the literal best first-aid kit at home. It's wondrous. It's got, like, twenty different kinds of bandages, real gauze, burn spray, antibiotic ointment, even a thermometer that talks. You'll be fixed up in no time."

That made me bark a quick ha-ha, a small, breathless sound that hurt my throat but eased something in my chest. "You're an unhinged angel. I'll take it."

Madison huffed but smiled, clearly relieved that I could still joke.

Carly, who'd been standing off to the side, finally stepped closer. Her mascara was smudged, and her voice shook when she spoke. "You scared the hell out of us, Claire." She swiped at her eyes. "But you're okay now. You're safe. I'm—I'm such an ass, I can't believe we fought earlier, I blame the alcohol, seriously, it messed with my head, I can't believe you almost died." Her run-on sentence ended in dramatic sniffles.

I looked up at her, her expression tight with guilt. "Carly, stop. It's fine. You didn't do anything wrong. I'm sorry for thinking even for one second it was you."

She shook her head stubbornly. "No, I did. I said things I didn't mean. I was just mad and stupid and— God, when I heard what happened, I thought . . ." Her voice cracked, and she pressed a hand to her mouth. "I thought I'd lost my best friend."

All I could do was nod. My throat still burned like hell, my pulse still felt too loud in my ears, but in that moment, I was anchored again.

Madison sat on the bumper of the ambulance closer to me, Carly hovered close, and Olivia inched nearer. The world, which had been spinning wildly just an hour ago, began to clear.

"Okay," I whispered, trying to steady my voice. "New rule. No more murder suspects, no more wine-fueled arguments, and no more near-death experiences."

Carly let out a watery laugh and wiped her snot with the back of her hand. "Deal."

Madison raised her hand like she was swearing an oath. "And I'm still bringing my first-aid kit."

"Of course you are," I said, smiling weakly. "Wouldn't expect anything less."

I tried to speak, but my throat tightened again. All that came out was a rasp of air.

Someone shouted something, startling me. The ambulance door slammed shut. I didn't even remember saying goodbye to Carly, Madison, and Olivia.

The paramedic adjusted the oxygen line, murmuring something about keeping still.

I wanted to tell them I was okay. That I just needed a minute. But my mind was detached, like it was still upstairs in that room, staring at all those photos and red Sharpie scrawls.

I caught fragments of voices drifting outdoors, murmurs spreading like wildfire through the crowd that had gathered at the edge of the driveway.

"They said he had a shrine to Bauer . . ."

"Did you hear? He framed Ava."

"He poisoned Liz Carper."

"A murderer. In Coral Haven. Can you believe that?"

The words echoed, disjointed and far away.

Coral Haven. My little beach town, full of farmers' markets and sunset concerts and gossiping shop owners, had an obsessive murderer among us.

I tried to rest and listened to the paramedic's voice blending with the static on the radio.

The steady feel of the ambulance's engine was the only thing holding me to the world. The siren wasn't blaring anymore, just a constant rhythm of tires over pavement and the occasional crackle of the radio.

I could feel every bump in the road through the stretcher, and each one sent a dull ache through my ribs and neck. My throat burned when I swallowed. The paramedic beside me adjusted something on the monitor, his face calm, practiced.

"You're doing great," he said quietly. "Not long now. We'll get you there soon."

The fluorescent lights above me blurred together, glowing halos that pulsed every time we hit a turn.

*

When we arrived outside the hospital, my body was trembling from fatigue. The rush of cooler wind hit me as they wheeled me out, the sound of the hospital blending into my fuzzy thoughts. Doors opening, voices echoing, the sharp scent of antiseptic.

Someone was asking for my name, my address, my insurance plan, my emergency contact numbers. I answered robotically, automatically, detached, like I was hearing someone else's voice.

They processed me quickly. CH General wasn't big, but it ran like a tight ship. Every nurse, every doctor seemed to already know what had happened, though no one said it outright.

After the X-rays and the blood pressure checks and the endless stream of gentle but relentless questions, they settled me in a single room. It was small, tidy, and smelled nice.

A thin moonbeam stretched across the floor, silver and soft.

On the small table beside my bed were two bright bouquets. One full of wildflowers, the other roses. A little card tucked between them read: *We love you, please rest —* *O, M & C.*

I smiled faintly, though it hurt to move my face.

The nurse dimmed the lights. "Your parents are on their way, sweetheart. They'll be here soon; within two to three hours," she said kindly. "Try to rest, okay?"

Rest.

I tried. I really did. But my mind wouldn't stop spiraling. Every flash of light, every sound from outside the door jolted me back into that bedroom, the shouting, the struggle, the photos on the wall.

It wasn't until nearly an hour later that I heard a quiet knock.

"Come in," I said, my voice scratchy.

The door opened, and Detective Hensley stepped inside.

She looked different out of chaos. Her hair pulled back neatly now, her jacket draped over one arm. There were faint dark circles under her eyes, the look of someone who hadn't slept in twenty-four hours and was running purely on adrenaline and coffee.

"Hey, Claire," she said softly. "How're you holding up?"

"I'm okay," I said, though the words came out more like a question than a statement. "Sore, but . . . here."

"That's what matters." She pulled up the chair beside my bed and sat down, exhaling. "You scared the hell out of me, you know that?"

I let out a shaky laugh. "You and me both. And apparently everyone else."

She smiled faintly, then her expression shifted, serious. "I wanted to come in person. I owe you the truth,

I want to tell you what happened. I usually don't believe in luck—but we were damn lucky with this one."

I sat up a little, the hospital sheets crinkling under me. "I remember you saying we had some catching up to do."

"Yes, we do." She leaned forward, elbows on her knees. "No fluff. Once we brought Ava in, things just didn't seem right. Everything started to unravel fast. She was terrified. Not by being caught, but by being framed. And honestly, I couldn't stop the feeling that she was telling the truth."

I stayed quiet, listening.

"For starters, Ava Delaney is in the clear. Her name's been officially cleared in both investigations. Liz Carper's and the one from her old job."

I blinked. "The one with her coworker?"

Hensley nodded. "We finally got a verified report from that case. Her coworker died of a sudden brain aneurysm. Natural causes. Ava had nothing to do with it. She just happened to be nearby when it happened, and office gossip did the rest."

The air left my chest in one long exhale I didn't realize I'd been holding. "So all this time . . ."

"She was running from a rumor," Hensley finished. "And she ran straight into another one."

Hensley continued, her voice low and even. "While Ava was being questioned, she told us about Adam. How he'd been around constantly, how he'd suggested making peace with Liz before the season started. He brought the gift—the wine and the balloon. Said it'd be a 'nice gesture.' Adam advised Ava to deliver the package to ease tension between her and Bauer. She did, thinking it would calm things between the shop rivalry and them."

I gulped. "Ava willingly delivered the poisoned wine, but she didn't know she was doing it?"

"Exactly. She had no idea the bottles were tampered with. Those wine bottles came straight from the Morgan family's stock—easy to access and mess with for Adam."

Hensley's tone hardened slightly. "The rat poison was traced to him too. Using his credit card history and receipts. We also found the same compound in Adam's backpack and closet that matched the residue in both bottles."

Then Hensley said, "Ava was released less than twenty-four hours after her arrest. There was no evidence of premeditation, and no motive that held up under scrutiny. Her story aligned perfectly once we started comparing timelines."

I swallowed hard. "And Adam?"

She sighed. "Once Ava was cleared, I immediately wanted to pay Adam a visit. Intuition. Regardless of what time it was."

Her eyes flicked to me, calm but filled with quiet anger. "I left the station to get a warrant and bring him in. I had a gut feeling something was off. That's why I went there. I was on my way when I heard calls come in about a disturbance at the Morgan Family Winery."

The image of her standing in that doorway, pulling Adam off me, flashed through my head. I felt a lump rise in my throat. I was extremely lucky.

"Thank you," I whispered, not knowing how to thank someone for saving my life.

She shook her head. "You don't need to thank me. You survived. That's all that matters."

Outdoors, a seagull cried, a faint, strange sound this late at night. Its squawk carried in from the dark water.

The hospital was quiet again.

"Claire," Hensley said at last, her voice softer now, stripped of its usual authority. "One more thing. We're almost certain that the suspicious call the hospital received—the one asking about Liz's condition—came from Adam. He was checking to see if his plan had worked. We cross-checked Adam's burner phone that was found in the closet. Number matches. Call time matches."

Her words seemed to hang there, stoic and sterile, like the air itself had stopped moving.

She studied me for a moment, her expression gentling. "You did something incredibly brave. You trusted your instincts, even when it put you in danger. Because of that, Liz gets justice. And Coral Haven . . ." She exhaled slowly. "Coral Haven finally gets a little peace."

"Peace," I repeated, my voice thin. The word was foreign in my mouth, too light for the weight it carried.

Hensley gave a small nod and stood, smoothing her jacket, the fabric whispering in the stillness. "Rest up. I'll be back tomorrow to take your full statement."

She paused at the door. "Your parents will be here soon."

I nodded, my eyes stinging. "Detective?"

She paused in the doorway. "Yeah?"

"What happens to Bauer now that he knows the truth?"

Her face softened. "He'll need time. They all will. And a good therapist." She hesitated, then gave me a small nod. "You did good, Claire. Thank you."

When the door closed, the silence filled the room again. The moonlight spilled across my blanket, soft and cool, and I let myself sink into it, finally letting my body feel the weight of everything that had happened. Outside my window, Coral Haven slept.

FIFTY

The moon had climbed higher by the time I woke up again, pale light dripping across the hospital room floor. The steady beep of the monitor and the drum of the air vent were the only sounds.

For a second, I thought I was alone. Then a familiar whisper broke the quiet.

"Okay, she's up. Don't cry again just yet."

I turned my head wincing a little, expecting to see my parents. Instead, it was Carly, Olivia, and Madison. Once more, they all crowded into the doorway like they didn't want to come in too fast and hurt me.

Madison rushed over first, her hair in a messy bun, her eyes rimmed with pink. "Jesus, Claire. You look like hell."

I laughed weakly. "Thanks. I feel it too."

Carly set a paper cup of coffee on my bedside table and leaned down to hug me gently. "We've been so worried. We've been pacing the waiting room for hours. They wouldn't let us in at first."

Olivia sniffled and brushed a tear off her cheek. "We told you this detective stuff was dangerous."

"Yeah," I croaked. "You did."

They snuggled closely, each of them touching some part of the bed or my blanket, as if making sure I was really there.

After a few moments of quiet, I asked, "How . . . how were there so many police officers there? I thought it was just Hensley?"

The three of them exchanged looks. Madison finally sighed. "Adam's mom."

"What about her?"

"She went into the house to use the bathroom right before everything went down," Olivia explained. "She said she heard yelling, something slamming upstairs, repeatedly. She knew his temper could be bad. I guess she'd seen glimpses of it before and she freaked out. She called 911 right away, telling them she heard an aggressive disturbance in her home."

Carly nodded. "And because town is literally five miles long, the cops showed up within minutes. Just as Detective Hensley was arriving. Total coincidence but thank fucking God for it."

My throat went tight. "I'm so lucky," I said in disbelief.

"Yeah," Madison said softly. "Pretty much."

None of us spoke. The silence wasn't uncomfortable, it was relieved, filling all the empty spaces where fear used to live.

Then Carly grinned suddenly. "You know, you owe us a birthday redo."

I grumbled, laughing despite the ache in my ribs. "You're not serious."

"Oh, we're serious," Olivia said, crossing her arms. "Maybe next time, we'll stick to brunch and a mimosa flight. Zero murderers invited."

That got a real laugh out of me. My chest hurt, but it felt good to laugh.

After they left, each hugging me three, then four times, promising to text when they got home, I sank back into the pillows, the flowers' perfume filling the room.

*

It wasn't long before I heard a familiar tone of voice. Then the door swung open.

"Claire!"

My mom's voice cracked on my name. She was crying before she even made it to the hospital bed, my dad right behind her, his face pale and drawn.

"Oh, sweetheart," she said, pulling me into a trembling hug. "We've been driving all night. We couldn't believe what we heard. I'm sorry we were so far away! How bad are you hurt? What did that boy do to you?"

I smiled faintly on her shoulder. "I'm okay, Mom. Really. Just a few bruises."

My dad's hand rested gently on my knee. "You scared the life out of us, kiddo."

"I scared myself," I admitted.

They both looked exhausted, like they hadn't stopped worrying since the phone rang. I was about to reassure them again when a brisk knock interrupted us.

A man in light-blue scrubs stepped in, reading from a clipboard. He was taller than I expected, maybe mid-thirties, dark hair slightly tousled, stubble he'd clearly given up on shaving halfway through the day. When he looked up, his smile was nice to look at. He was handsome.

"Ms. Collins?" he said. "I'm Dr. Miquella. I'm just finishing your chart and thought I'd update everyone before you try to make an escape."

My mom straightened, instantly protective. "Is she alright?"

He nodded. "Considering what happened, Claire is very lucky. Mild concussion, extensive bruising along the clavicle and jawline, and some strain to the neck and upper back muscles. Several superficial abrasions on her arms, and mild lacerations to her foot from broken glass. She needed a few stitches, but nothing deep."

He glanced down at the chart before continuing. "No fractures, no internal bleeding, and her oxygen levels are back to normal."

He glanced at me, raising an eyebrow. "Which means plenty of rest, hydration, and patience. Ice for the swelling, alternating with gentle heat after the first twenty-four hours. Change and clean your bandages for the wounds. No lifting anything heavier than a notebook for a week. You may feel stiff or dizzy for a few days, but that's expected."

Mom still looked unconvinced. "You're sure that's all?"

Dr. Miquella smiled again. "Her vitals are steady. She put up a good fight, from what the EMTs tell me."

"Damn right I fucking did," I muttered, my voice raspier than I meant it to be.

He laughed quietly. "I can tell. You should see the other guy."

That made Dad's eyebrows rise. "Is he in the hospital?"

"No," the doctor said, tone turning professional again. "Minor injuries only. He was treated at the scene and taken into custody. You don't need to worry about him being anywhere near you."

The knot in my stomach loosened a little. "Good," I breathed. "I was afraid he'd show up here."

"Not a chance," Dr. Miquella said. "You're safe."

"Now, I'm recommending plenty of fluids, light meals, and rest. Think of it as a bad vacation. You'll be tired. Let your body do the work. And if you get headaches, blurred vision, or nausea that won't quit, come back in. Otherwise, take it slow."

Mom nodded solemnly, as if she'd just been handed marching orders. "We'll make sure of it."

"I'll have the nurse bring an extra set of instructions before you're discharged." He looked at me again, eyes bright with a trace of mischief. "And for the record, if you ever get bored of blogging, you'd make a decent boxer."

I grinned, wincing slightly at the stretch in my neck. "Maybe I'll start a new column—'How Not to Get Strangled in a Beach Town.'"

He chuckled and showed his dashing smile. "I'd read that."

When he left, it seemed like the panic had ushered out with him.

My mom reached for my hand again. "He's cute! I'll get you his number," she said. "You should come home with us, or at least let us stay close for a bit. Just until things calm down."

"I might," I said. "But I'll be okay. I promise."

*

They stayed a while longer, holding my hands, asking a dozen questions I could barely answer. Eventually their voices softened, steadied. Before they left, Mom kissed my forehead.

"We'll be waiting at your place tomorrow," she said. "We just want to make sure you're really okay."

"I will be," I said, and meant it.

When the door finally closed again, I was alone with the steady beeping of the heart-rate monitor. Beep, beep, beep.

I cupped my hands in front of me, pretending there was a candle there. One lonely little flame for my birthday that had gone wildly off script. I blew it out, slow and steady, and wished for something simple.

Less drama.

Then I just lay there, staring up at the ceiling, letting the weight of the last twenty-four hours settle in. Ava, wrongly accused. My birthday turned nightmare. Adam, twisted, obsessed, dangerous. And Liz, finally getting justice.

Somewhere out there, Bauer was going to hear what happened. I wondered how it would break him. How it would affect him.

I exhaled, long and slow, my chest rising and falling like the tide. The town needed a break. A long, quiet, off-season kind of break.

And so did I.

FIFTY-ONE

Three days had passed since everything happened. The lights, the sirens, the shouts, and the front-page headlines all seemed like a fever dream.

I was curled up on my couch, cocooned in my big black fluffy blanket, a mug of tea balanced on the coffee table. Candles flickered along the windowsill. The TV was playing one of my comfort shows, nothing too heavy, just something familiar enough to make me forget the ache in my ribs for a while. Every time I shifted or laughed too hard, I felt the dull sting of bruises deep beneath the surface.

But I was alive. And that was enough.

Mom had decided to stay with me for a while, just until I was fully back on my feet. She'd come home with me from the hospital, suitcase in hand, already fussing over the state of my kitchen. The next morning, she made her famous Italian wedding soup. It simmered for hours, filling the apartment with the smell of garlic, broth, and fresh parsley. I hadn't realized how much I'd missed that smell until it hit me. We ate curled up on the couch, bowls balanced on our knees, a blanket around both of us. When the credits rolled on the movie we were watching, she just reached over and smoothed my hair, whispering something about how she'd never seen anyone so brave. I quietly drifted off to sleep.

*

In the days that followed, my phone barely stopped buzzing.

Neighbors. Friends. People I hadn't spoken to in months. Each message was a mix of worry and gratitude. Checking in, making sure I was okay, thanking me for being "so brave." The word *brave* didn't sit right with me, but I appreciated the kindness behind it.

A delivery came soon after. A bouquet of white lilies and soft blue hydrangeas with a neat envelope tucked into the stems.

It was from Liz's parents.

The note inside was handwritten, the ink pressed deep into the paper. *Thank you for helping bring the truth to light. Liz would have wanted someone like you in her corner.*

I must have read it a dozen times before setting it on my desk beside my mug of cold tea.

*

In other news, Bauer and Ava were stronger than ever. They'd already announced plans to reopen their shop under a new name, with new inventory and a fresh coat of optimism. The white awnings and gold-lettered signage went up almost overnight, clean and elegant. A promise that life could start over.

Part of me admired them for it. Another part wondered if this was how people survived here: by sanding down the past until it shined again. They weren't villains, just two people who had lost more than they could have admitted. Misunderstood. Human. However, some people never face consequences in court — only in the quiet knowledge that they stood beside something evil and survived it.

There was talk of a memorial bench being installed on Beach Street, right outside Liz's old storefront. People had already started leaving flowers, seashells, and small notes beneath candles that burned down to soft puddles of colorful wax by morning. I walked by earlier that week and saw a child's bracelet looping gently around one of the temporary wooden slats. What a simple, quiet act of love.

Coral Haven had lost someone they loved and learned just how fragile trust could be in a town this small.

The sky outside had gone from silver to deep blue, the last trace of daylight slipping beneath the dunes. My tea nearly finished, but untouched for an hour.

I pulled my laptop closer, the soft glow lighting the folds of my blanket. A fresh draft waited on the screen. My fingers hovered over the keys for a long moment, unsure where to start. So much had already been said already. In headlines, in whispers, in everything that couldn't be undone.

But this time, I wasn't writing for them.

I was writing for me.
And I started to type.

*

This Week on the Dunes: A Season of Shadows and Sunlight

A Different Kind of Season

It's hard to put into words what these last few months have been like.

Coral Haven has always felt like its own little bubble — sunsets, surfboards, and stories that usually end with laughter and salt in our hair. The kind of place where the biggest worry is whether you remembered sunscreen.

But this season... we saw something much darker drift to shore.

Remembering Liz

We lost someone who meant a great deal to this town.

Liz Carper wasn't perfect — none of us are — but she was part of the heartbeat of Coral Haven. Her shop wasn't just a store; it was a meeting place, a memory-maker. You could walk in for a candle and leave with a conversation.

Even in tragedy, she managed to bring the community together one last time.

The Truth, At Last

Thanks to the tireless work of Detective Natalie Hensley and the Coral Haven Police Department, Liz's story finally has answers. The truth surfaced.

It's shaken us, yes. But it reminded us of something important: how strong this town can be when it must be.

What Comes Next

As the season winds down and the beach grows quiet again, I hope we carry that same closeness forward. Coral Haven has always been more than pretty views and postcard moments.

It's people. It's heart. It's resilience.

Because when storms pass, Coral Haven does what it always does:

We rebuild.

—Claire Bear

*

I sat back and reread the post, the laptop light mixing with the candlelight. The words felt final this time and not in a sad way, but in the way endings sometimes feel when they've been waiting to happen.

Outside, the waves kept rolling in steadily and patiently, indifferent to everything that had unfolded on the shore. Somewhere down Beach Street, I thought I heard laughter, faint and human and alive. I smiled.

I closed my laptop and let the quiet settle around me. The candles flickered, their light dancing across the walls, turning the small apartment golden. I pulled the blanket tighter over my shoulders and breathed in scents of salt, wax, and peace.

On the coffee table sat my old storyboard, worn edges covered in scribbled notes. I reached for it, smoothing out the page where I'd left earlier that summer, back before everything changed. The pen was strangely familiar in my hand.

Maybe it was time to start again. Not as the blogger chasing stories, but as the writer telling her own.

Epilogue

This Week on the Dunes: September Reflections: A Town Exhales

It's been a strange, quiet kind of September here in Coral Haven. The summer crowds have thinned, the boardwalk's gone still, and for the first time in months, the town feels like it can breathe again.

Justice and the Waiting Game

Adam Morgan remains in custody, awaiting trial. His attorney has entered an insanity plea—a last attempt to explain what so many of us still can't make sense of. Some days, it feels like justice is on its way. Other days, it just feels like another story no one wants to tell anymore.

Love and Linen at The Shore Thing

Meanwhile, Ava and Bauer are back at the revamped store, and business is somehow better than ever—even in the first week of the off-season. Their new fall display, all linen neutrals and gold leaf, looks like it belongs in a glossy magazine. Talk on the street is, Bauer's planning to pop a question soon. The two of them have been inseparable—a picture-perfect couple emerging with the calm after the storm.

Fall in Coral Haven

The fall festival's right around the corner: pumpkin carvings, the Halloween parade, hayrides out by the farms, and cider donut stands returning to Beach Street. The air smells like cinnamon again.

A Farewell for Now

As for me, I'll be stepping back from my weekly posts for a while. Maybe it's time to trade the late-night edits and coffee-fueled deadlines for something gentler—stories meant for smaller hands and bigger imaginations. Keep an eye out for my children's books at your local library (fingers crossed).

Until next time, Coral Haven—thank you for reading, for caring, and for letting me tell your stories.

XOXO

—Claire Bear

Acknowledgments

This book would not exist without my husband, David. Thank you for your endless love, patience, and unwavering support. For always listening to my completely nonsensical monologues, reading the very early (and very questionable) pieces I started with, and never once making me feel weird or dumb for dreaming big. You've been my best friend for over a decade, and I wouldn't be who I am, or as successful in love and life without you.

To my children, Deacon and Ryann, the real MVPs. Thank you for your constant companionship, emotional support, and for "helping" type this book by sitting directly on my shoulders and feet at the most inconvenient times. Your contributions did not go unnoticed. Big stretch!

To my parents, siblings, and in-laws: Thank you for listening, encouraging, and nodding quietly and politely while I explained my ideas. No matter how dark, dramatic, or half-formed they were at the time, you all persevered. Your support means more than you know.

A special thank you to my dad for our editing and productivity meetings. Your feedback, patience, and willingness to dig into the details with me meant a lot. And to Emily, for reading through the first edition.

And to Dillyn, an incredibly talented graphic designer. Thank you for helping design the book spine and back cover. Your vision, creativity, and attention to detail brought this story to life in a way I could only imagine.

To my editor, Madison Schultz, your insight, knowledge, patience, and hard work turned this story into something readable (and something I'm incredibly proud of). It was a true pleasure working with you.

To my Cape May club and Book Clerb—thank you for enduring my endless TLDR texts, my ungodly morbid ideas, and my late-night sticker spamming. Your honesty, humor, and emotional support helped keep me grounded and helped carry this book across the finish line.

Thank you to Nicole and Steve for your constant encouragement and for being a source of inspiration and ideas along the way.

And to all the family and friends who read versions one, two, three, four (and beyond) your time, feedback, and belief in this story meant everything to me.

And finally, to you, the reader—thank you for picking up this book and spending time in Coral Haven. THANK YOU FOR YOUR SUPPORT! I hope the mystery kept you guessing, the characters stayed with you, and the read was worth it.

This book was built with love, patience, and an incredible village behind it. Thank you all for helping make it possible.

What Happened to Liz — Book Club Discussion Questions

1. **Trust and Perception:**
   Coral Haven appears close-knit and idyllic on the surface. How did the town's culture of familiarity and trust both protect and endanger its residents throughout the story?

2. **The Role of the Observer:**
   Claire begins the novel as a blogger and observer rather than an active participant. How does her role evolve, and do you think her involvement ultimately helps or complicates the search for truth?

3. **Appearances vs. Reality:**
   Several characters are not who they initially seem to be. Which revelation surprised you the most, and why? Were there moments in hindsight that hinted at the truth?

4. **Justice and Closure:**
   By the end of the novel, justice takes different forms for different characters. Did the resolution feel satisfying to you? Why or why not?

5. **Community After Tragedy:**
   How do you think Coral Haven will remember Liz after the events of the book? Do you believe communities truly heal after loss, or do they simply learn how to live alongside it?

www.ingramcontent.com/pod-product-compliance
Lightning Source LLC
LaVergne TN
LVHW091718070526
838199LV00050B/2444